# GUNS OF THE GAMBLER

Destitute gambler Ben Crow arrives in Mallory keen to claim his inheritance, only to discover that rancher Edward Bacon has other ideas. Set up by Miss Dorothy, who had fooled him completely, Ben finds himself dangling at the end of a rope. Saved from death, Ben sets off in pursuit of Miss Dorothy, determined upon retribution. However, his quest for vengeance turns into a rescue mission when she is kidnapped by a crazy man-burning bandit.

# M. DUGGAN

# GUNS OF THE GAMBLER

*Complete and Unabridged*

# LINFORD
*Leicester*

First published in Great Britain in 1998 by
Robert Hale Limited
London

First Linford Edition
published 1999
by arrangement with
Robert Hale Limited
London

British Library CIP Data

Duggan, M.
    Guns of the gambler.—Large print ed.—
Linford western library
    1. Western stories
    2. Large type books.
    I. Title
    823.9'14 [F]

    ISBN 0-7089-5491-X

Published by
F. A. Thorpe (Publishing) Ltd.
Anstey, Leicestershire

Set by Words & Graphics Ltd.
Anstey, Leicestershire
Printed and bound in Great Britain by
T. J. International Ltd., Padstow, Cornwall

This book is printed on acid-free paper

# 1

Edward Bacon stared at the small log cabin which lay below and then his gaze shifted to the buggy which stood before the cabin. He recognized the buggy. Only one person in Mallory drove a buggy which had been painted bright red. That person was the doctor. As Bacon watched, an old Mexican moved slowly across the yard. Bacon smiled contemptuously; anyone other than Samuel Church would have fired the arthritic oldster, but no, Church had kept him around. Bacon did not carry 'dead wood' as he called those employees past their usefulness.

Bacon glanced at the man beside him, his ramrod Meaks. As always, Meaks's ugly face with its broken nose, was impassive. But Meaks was a predictable man. Bacon remained unconcerned as to what Meaks might

1

be thinking. Not much, he would have said if asked. Meaks was a man content to obey orders which made him the ideal ramrod.

'Looks like Miss Dorothy has company,' Meaks observed quite unnecessarily.

Bacon snorted.

'It's only to be expected she's been taken poorly,' Meaks continued doggedly, with a sideways glance at Bacon. 'Considering what she's been through.' A taciturn man today, Meaks was behaving uncharacteristically.

Without troubling to respond to Meaks's foolishness, Bacon dug in his gold star spurs and started downwards leaving Meaks to follow or not as he chose. Shale slid beneath the hooves of the rancher's grey. Bacon did not anticipate problems. Miss Dorothy could not run a goddamn sheep ranch and anyone fool enough to hire out to her would not last long. Bacon had been systematically scaring off Sam Church's men. Some were beaten-up in town; some found

2

themselves the recipients of a sniper's bullet — the first time was a warning; the second time it was always serious, leaving men disabled or dead.

Bacon allowed himself to smile. Miss Dorothy wouldn't know one end of a woolly from the other. Samuel Church had possessed decided views upon a woman's place. Church's land was as good as his. No one else would be so foolish as to put in a bid.

Bacon had also seen to it that the general store would continue to demand cash. There would be no credit for Miss Dorothy should she be so foolish as to request it. Folk in Mallory would continue to look the other way. Why, the woman would be darn glad to accept his offer, grateful that he had made it.

As Bacon, with his ramrod following behind him, reached the ranch house, as if on cue, Doc's short, portly figure emerged from the house. He glared at the two men, aware why Edward Bacon had come calling. Doc was one of the few people who did not fear Bacon. Even Bacon, unprincipled polecat that he was, recognized that some time in the future he might find himself in urgent need of a doctor's services.

'I figured you'd be showing up sooner or later,' Doc stated without preamble.

'Good day to you, Doc,' Bacon responded pleasantly, as he dismounted. He stood for a moment, sunlight striking silver hair, a still handsome man despite hitting his middle fifties. Doc caught a whiff of cologne.

Meaks, with his weather-lined face, smelt of sweat and horses. Doc found himself wondering whether it had been Meaks who had beaten Samuel Church's head to an unrecognizable pulp having first crept up behind the snoozing oldster as he had fished down at the creek. Despite his troubles, old Sam had continued to fish as if defying Bacon to do something about it. Well, someone had and there had been no man-hunt to track down the drifter

Bacon and the sheriff maintained had been responsible. Miss Dorothy, of course, had been in no position to insist upon anything.

'Couldn't wait for the earth to settle, huh?' Doc jibed. 'You must want old Sam's land powerful bad.'

'Keep your nose out of my affairs,' Bacon responded coldly.

Unexpectedly, Doc grinned. 'Go on in, Bacon, I'll just smoke myself a cigar whilst you're about your business. I'm in no particular hurry to leave.'

'Stay here, Meaks.' Bacon took the words at face value. He strode inside.

Meaks watched as the little doctor puffed away at a fat cigar. 'You look pleased,' he essayed.

'It's about time Bacon got his come-uppance,' Doc responded. 'Old Sam has outsmarted that conniving crook; ain't no way Bacon is going to get Sam's land without one hell of a fight. It stands to reason that Sam wouldn't have left this place to a pliable *hombre*. I reckon Sam had a reason for cutting

Miss Dorothy out of his will, and that reason concerned your no-account boss, Edward Bacon.'

'You mean . . . ' Meaks began.

'Not a cent. He ain't left his granddaughter a darn cent. That's why I'm here. Quite naturally, Dorothy temporarily lost her senses. I've had to sedate her. The minister's wife is with her now.'

'Then who the hell owns the place?' Meaks demanded.

'Some *hombre* ain't none of us heard of, an Easterner answering to the handle of Bradley Crowther the Third.'

Meaks whistled. 'Crowther the Third had best see sense or his health will suffer,' he observed.

'Well, I hope he don't,' Doc snapped. 'What we need hereabouts is a man as rotten as Bacon himself.'

'Can you spare a cigar?' Wisely Meaks did not pursue Doc's last remark.

'I can't. I'm particular who I smoke with,' Doc said. 'No goddamn drifter killed old Sam; the whole town knows it and I guess you know it too.'

'I know nothing,' Meaks responded, a muscle beneath his left eye twitching.

★ ★ ★

'You can't see her.' The minister's wife barred Bacon's path. 'It's not decent.'

Bacon snorted. 'Don't talk foolishness, ma'am. I've been in a lady's bedroom before. I mean, Mrs Bacon's,' he added hurriedly, seeing the fool woman's expression.

As the minister's wife, with evident reluctance, moved aside, Bacon, squaring his shoulders, entered Miss Dorothy's bedroom anticipating with pleasure the outraged squeal she would utter upon seeing a man in her bedroom. He was disappointed; Miss Dorothy didn't move, just lay there, eyes shut, tucked up to the chin. Only then did Bacon give a thought to the upturned stools and smashed crockery. Someone had hurled an apple pie at the wall. He was conscious of the woman beside him twisting her apron.

'Poor Dorothy became quite deranged when she heard the terrible news.'

'She looked just fine at her grandpa's funeral,' Bacon rejoined.

'Not that news. It's the will I refer to. Poor Samuel must have been losing his wits for he has left it all, this ranch and his sheep, to some Easterner or other. Poor Dorothy has never heard of the man. Quite naturally she was quite overcome . . . '

Bacon, face suffusing with fury, shoved past the twittering female and rushed outside. He gulped air and cussed beneath his breath as he fought an urge to throttle Doc. Doc had known, of course.

'It appears to me you've had a wasted journey,' Doc observed jovially.

'Why, you — '

Quickly, Meaks stepped between the two men. 'Ain't no use you blaming the doc,' he stated softly. 'It's this Bradley Crowther the Third you've got to start thinking about. Maybe the *hombre* will sell up without ever setting foot in Mallory.'

'I wouldn't bet on it.' Doc clambered aboard his buggy and flicked the reins. 'Maybe I'll be seeing you in a professional capacity, Bacon,' he jibed, as the buggy moved away.

'Only a darn fool lays violent hands on a damn fine doctor. Ain't no telling when any one of us will need the man,' Meaks reasoned. 'Take myself, for example, if I'm in line to take a slug I need to know there's a doc around to put me right. And that goes for the rest of the men.'

Bacon recovered himself. He shook away Meaks's restraining hand. 'We're not talking about a ranch war here, Meaks. This Easterner . . .'

'This Bradley Crowther the Third,' Meaks filled in helpfully.

'This Easterner,' Bacon gritted his teeth, 'is but the one man. I feel sure he can be persuaded to see reason. I'll have a word in town; when Crowther the Third arrives I intend to be there to personally welcome him to Mallory.'

★ ★ ★

Bradley Crowther the Third, more commonly known as plain Ben Crow, leaned back against the upholstery. He was in the Mallory-bound stage reeking of whiskey and cigar fumes much to the ill-concealed disgust of the smartly suited *hombre* sitting opposite him. Ben knew the man to be a missionary on leave from the Sandwich Islands, wherever they might be, bound for Mallory to stay with his brother the town's minister.

Ben had declined to volunteer any information concerning himself. He could have said he was a successful gambling man in dire straits due to an act of Christian charity. He doubted whether he would have been believed. He did not look successful nor the sort to go in for Christian charity. He looked, at present, like a no-account, drunken bum.

Something stank and Ben was not referring to the stage. He guessed he would find out what it might be as soon as he reached Mallory. Old Samuel Church had not left him a sizeable, prosperous spread out of the goodness of his old heart.

Ben had heard the name. Samuel Church had been an acquaintance of Ben's grandfather, the first Bradley Crowther. There'd been some scandal. Grandpa had been accused of embezzlement and the righteous accuser had been good old Samuel Church. And now, old Sam Church had named the grandson of the man he had denounced as his beneficiary. It had occurred to Ben as he had downed his whiskey that maybe old Sam was out to get him. Sam Church couldn't have known that Bradley Crowther the Third was operating as the gambler and sometimes gun-sharp Ben Crow. Or could he? Ben deliberated as the stage brought him nearer to Mallory.

' 'Trust ye not in man but trust in the Lord',' the minister's brother concluded, unaware that Ben had not been listening to the rambling account of saved souls.

Ben tipped back his hat. 'Sure is hotter than Hell,' he drawled, biting back the retort that he himself preferred to trust in his good old Colt .45. It had never let him down yet and upon more than one occasion had kept the peace.

'No earthly fire can compare to the fire of Hell,' his travelling companion rebuked.

'I reckon not.' Ben shook his head as he heard the driver yell out they'd be hitting Mallory in about five minutes. He was drunk, but not so drunk he could not haul iron. Fortuitously he'd always been able to hold his liquor.

Once again, Ben asked himself what he was doing in Mallory. He was not a ranching man. A gentleman gambler was how he would have described himself. Anyone seeing him in his down-at-heel boots and worn duds would have hooted with laughter. Ben thinned his lips; his presence in Mallory was solely due to his one-time partner, the Italian Angelo Linelli. The man had been born here and ought to have known better than to fall foul of the authorities in Mexico, particularly when a fellow Italian was in command of the fort.

Hearing Linelli was in a Spanish hell-hole, Ben had crossed the border, it being in his mind that maybe there was a way to save Linelli before they shot him.

And it had been De Bois, the fort commander, who had approached Ben, coolly informing him that he knew why Ben was here.

'Why die for nothing?' De Bois had asked. The bastard had known to the last cent what Ben was worth. He'd even taken Ben's gambling suits and new boots. But De Bois had kept his word, Linelli had escaped from the fort, neither had he been the first.

'You have your ranch,' Linelli had said.

'Get out of my sight you jackass,' Ben had replied furiously. 'I'm wiped out. I ought to have let them shoot you. Just get, before I plug you myself.' Wisely Linelli had forked it out pretty damn quick.

'The minister's brother huh!' Ben drawled mockingly. 'Then I can count on you should I need a handout, Christian charity and all that!'

'I, er — ' With alacrity, Ben's travelling companion opened the stage door as the vehicle came to a jarring halt.

'I guess not,' Ben observed drily. Hell his head was aching as though the Devil himself were pounding him. It would be lukewarm beer from now on. Leastways whilst he remained in Mallory. First thing he'd best discover was how old Sam Church had died. If it was not of natural causes, Ben guessed he'd best watch his back.

'Welcome to Mallory, Mr Crowther,' a resonant voice boomed. 'Allow me to introduce myself. I'm Edward Bacon, your neighbour.'

Ben smiled drily. This he had to see. As he stepped down from the stage the sunlight struck him almost as if it were a physical blow. Ben stumbled and grabbed the swinging stage door for support. That settled it, no more whiskey. Raising his head he looked at the scene before him, the hairs of his neck bristling the way they did when he sensed trouble heading his way.

A large number of folk had turned out to meet the Mallory stage. Ben recognized the expressions: avid interest; suppressed excitement; disapproval. He'd seen them all before. Folk congregated when trouble was brewing and trouble was no stranger to Ben Crow.

But for once eyes were not upon him. He was being ignored. Attention was fixed upon the smart, large, distinguished, silver-headed man who was even now holding out his hand for the man he thought to be Bradley Crowther the Third.

'There's been a mistake . . . ' the minister's brother began, but Bacon did not allow him to finish.

'There certainly has. Old Sam had agreed to sell me his land. I assume you'll want to honour his last wishes.' So saying Bacon seized hold of the missionary's right hand.

The veins in Bacon's temple throbbed and the missionary's face contorted with pain as the man struggled not to cry out. A fine way to welcome a *hombre* Ben thought, mangle his gun hand and then issue an ultimatum. He felt he ought to take off his hat to Edward Bacon. And he'd eat that hat if old Sam Church had died of natural causes.

'I've had a Bill of Sale drawn up,' Bacon continued. 'I'm convinced you'll find my offer fair and generous.' He did not release the missionary's hand. Nor had Bacon travelled to town alone. Ben's eyes scanned the hard-faced waddies who were obviously in Bacon's employ. One in particular, an ugly galoot with a broken nose and thinning hair. The ramrod Ben assumed.

Meaks stared at the bum. A faint breeze carried the scent of whiskey which emanated from the man. Thirty or thereabouts, Meaks thought, his eyes dropping to the pearl-handled guns the bum wore tied low to the leg, gunfighter fashion. It was rare these days to see a two-gun man. The thought came to Meaks that a no-account saddle-bum ought not to be wearing two guns.

The bum's eyes were mocking, Meaks saw. He could not see much of the man's face because it was covered with stubble.

Deciding it was time to put an end to this farce, Ben stepped forward. His voice was hoarse but steady. 'I'll thank you kindly, Bacon, to release my travelling companion.' He paused.

'And if you ain't of a mind to release the minister's brother just returned from saving heathen souls, well, I guess I'll have to persuade you.'

The bum had an odd sense of humour Meaks thought. And evidently didn't think much of men of the cloth, albeit he might be needing one soon for Bacon did not take kindly to being bad mouthed.

'The minister's brother!' Bacon dropped the hand as though it had turned red hot. 'Why in tarnation didn't you say, man?'

'He would have done if you hadn't been doing your darnedest to put his gun hand out of action,' Ben drawled.

'Who the hell are you? I'll be damned if I'll take insult from a no-account drunk.'

To Ben's amusement, folk began to move out of the line of fire. He felt strangely detached from all this. He guessed it was the whiskey. And he'd been in tricky situations similar to this more times than he could remember.

Nor did he particularly care if his luck ran out.

Dimly, Meaks recognized that the bum facing down Edward Bacon didn't give a damn either way, which made him even more dangerous.

The telegraph was a marvellous invention and a telegraph had confirmed that Bradley Crowther the Third would be arriving in Mallory on this very stage. Bacon was clearly assuming Crowther the Third had missed the stage. Meaks had never judged men by the smart suits they wore. So, if pin-stripe suit was not Crowther the Third that only left one other.

Meaks stepped between the two men. 'I believe, Mr Bacon,' he said, as respectfully as he could, although he was fighting to keep a straight face, 'that you'll find you're talking to Bradley Crowther the Third.'

'You're loco, Meaks.' Bacon dismissed the assumption with a snort.

'Would anyone care to tell me,' Ben addressed no one in particular, 'just

19

what happened to Samuel Church? Just how come he ended planted six feet under?'

'Why, someone stove in the back of poor Sam's skull,' a voice from the back of the crowd yelled out. 'They used a rock on him. He was getting on and liked a snooze down by the creek. He was told time and time again it weren't safe, what with his hands being shot at and beaten. 'You'll be next', I told him. But he paid me no mind and paid the price for his folly.'

'Mighty interesting,' Ben observed. 'As old Sam's beneficiary I've been wondering all the way to Mallory what happened to the old Bible thumper. I guess that puts my mind at rest. I find it trying not knowing what I'm up against. When it comes to shaking hands if you don't mind, Mr Bacon, I'll pass. And as for your Bill of Sale, only the fact that there are ladies present prevents me from telling you to what use it could best be put.'

'I know you, son.' A gnarled oldster pushed his way to the fore. 'I've seen you in action way back. Bradley Crowther the Third, you say. When I saw you, you were answering to the handle of Ben Crow.'

# 2

'Well it sure beats being called Bradley Crowther the Third,' Ben drawled. Someone at the back of the crowd laughed. Edward Bacon's expression changed. Intimidating a tenderfoot called Crowther the Third was one thing; intimidating Crow the gambler and fast gun was another. Ben waited, knowing the wheels inside Bacon's devious, conniving mind were turning.

Finally, Bacon, throwing back his head, gave a loud guffaw. 'I can't see you nursemaiding a bunch of stinking sheep, Mr Crow,' he remarked almost jovially. 'Perhaps you'd care to discuss terms over at the Buffalo Head saloon. I'm a generous man. Sell out to me and you can be on your way just like that.' Bacon snapped his fingers as if to emphasize his point.

Sam Church, Ben saw now, had

played the bottom card. Hell, he'd been left a sheep ranch. No way could Ben see himself as a sheep man; a prosperous rancher, yes, but sheepherder, never. He almost agreed there and then to follow Bacon to the Buffalo Head, but he smelt a rat, Bacon was too eager to get his hands on old Sam's land. And had not Bacon, a moment before, publicly labelled Ben a bum? Besides, he'd been told he'd been born obstinate.

'Don't that beat all,' Ben drawled, aware the spectators were watching, some of them plainly anticipating a showdown. 'I guess that old buzzard, Church, must be laughing in Hell. You must want that land real bad, Mr Bacon, seeing as you've ridden in especially to greet the stage. I guess I'll just have to mull things over awhile.'

Bacon stiffened. Ben knew Bacon was a man on a short rein, but Bacon contented himself with a curt nod. 'There's no immediate urgency, Crow. I'll admit I've expansion in mind.' He paused. 'And like all cattlemen I'd like to see the sheep gone from Mallory. But you take your time, Mr Crow. I'll drop by in a few days time after you've had a chance to accustom yourself to the woollies.' He turned to his men. 'Come on you no-good varmints, wet your whistle at my expense.'

Loud whoops and cheers greeted this announcement. Assuming a grin, Bacon led his men towards the Buffalo Head. He'd managed to back down without losing face, no mean feat Ben knew.

'I'm Walt Rudkin,' the oldster introduced himself. 'Owner of the livery barn,' he added, with some pride.

'Pleased to meet you, Walt.' Ben shook the gnarled hand. 'I guess I'll be needing a horse.' His lips compressed; truth was he was not now in a hurry to see his inheritance.

'You'll need a fast mover to keep ahead of Bacon,' Walt advised. 'Plenty around here believe he knows more

24

about Sam's demise than he's letting on.'

'What do you think?' Ben enquired, matching his stride to that of the oldster.

'I can't rightly say. Stoving in old Sam's skull wouldn't trouble Bacon none for he's a black-hearted varmint.' They walked on in silence until they reached the livery barn. 'Care to share a jug before riding out to view your inheritance?' Walt suggested. 'You'll need fortifying before you face Miss Dorothy, old Sam's spinster granddaughter. Her face puts me in mind of sour lemons, for she has that look about her.'

'No drink except black coffee,' Ben rejoined. 'As Bacon wants the land powerful bad I'd best keep my wits about me, wouldn't you say?'

'I guess,' Rudkin agreed. 'Although as you ain't turned him down flat he has no reason to drygulch you yet awhile. Sit yourself down and I'll cook up bacon and beans. Once you get out to the ranch you'll eat nothing but mutton and corn cakes. Sure is bad how old Sam cut the girl out of his will and left it all to you. But then, I guess he wanted someone around with the skill to blast Bacon, despatch him to a better place you could say.'

Ben sat. He was learning plenty from the garrulous oldster Rudkin.

'You would not believe the misfortune which has befallen old Sam's men. Drygulched some of them, shot dead mostly or beaten by drunken waddies in town. Those Mexicans disappeared faster than snow in August.'

Sitting before the livery barn, Ben was content to watch as Rudkin kindled a fire. He was hungry. He guessed he could manage bacon and beans and then he would head for the bath house and a long, hot soak.

'In the event of your demise the property reverts to Miss Dorothy,' Rudkin continued.

'Maybe old Sam was hopeful Bacon and myself would blast each other into

Kingdom Come,' Ben essayed.

'That sounds like the man I knew,' Rudkin agreed, throwing bacon into the pan. 'Now Miss Dorothy I'd say would want to sell out. That's just my opinion now. Old Sam would be turning in his grave,' Rudkin ruminated. He threw a glance at Ben. 'She's a lady; mind you treat her like one. She ain't your sort.'

Ben shrugged. 'Miss Dorothy is free to go or stay as she pleases. I ain't making a decision until I've seen all the cards.'

'Miss Dorothy was taken poorly following the loss of her grandpa,' Rudkin continued, without looking directly at Ben.

Ben concentrated on his bacon and beans praying that Rudkin wasn't implying that Miss Dorothy had gone crazy. He'd seen a crazy woman once. During a particularly hard winter she had lost three young ones. When Ben had seen her she'd been just sitting there, rocking, unable to feed or cleanse herself, quite oblivious to the fact that her desperate husband planned to ship her to an asylum. 'Do you want the job of escorting her?' he'd asked Ben in sheer desperation. 'Hell will freeze over before I am party to such a deed,' Ben had rejoined.

'There's poorly and poorly,' Ben essayed.

Rudkin grunted by way of a response. 'Minister says she's fine now but just tread carefully around Miss Dorothy.'

'Damnation.' Ben found he had quite lost his appetite.

★ ★ ★

Two weeks hence found Ben chafing at the bit. He'd despatched a missive to a good friend in Washington; being a Crowther he still possessed connections of a sort. If a railroad was heading through Mallory he'd soon know. Of necessity, he'd been forced to help Miss Dorothy's sole remaining hand, an arthritic old Mexican who'd chosen to stay around. Such honest work had left him feeling not well pleased as his aunt would have said. Mercifully, Miss Dorothy, the sour-faced spinster of some thirty years or more, had proved as sane as Ben himself. Given her penury she had taken it upon herself to act as housekeeper. She was a tolerable cook and baked a fine apple pie he had discovered. Not feeling at ease around Miss Dorothy and at her suggestion, Ben had been willing to bunk down in what had been the bunkhouse. There'd been no sign of Edward Bacon. No longer feeling pressured into selling, Ben had determined that upon discovering the true value of Church land he would be prepared to sell. He'd also determined to split fifty-fifty with Miss Dorothy. Ben Crow, it seemed, possessed a conscience after all. As for the murder of old Sam, as Miss Dorothy had not raised the subject, Ben, mindful of Rudkin's words, had kept his lips buttoned.

Having fixed the roof which had been leaking, Ben rolled himself a smoke. Miss Dorothy had taken the buggy and gone into town for church worship. They'd eat when she returned. As Rudkin had warned it would be mutton.

Ben stared up at the sky. Clear blue with soft balls of white. Unbidden words which he had once read came into his mind. 'A good day to die,' the fictitious character had said.

In the distance, he saw the approaching speck which was Miss Dorothy's buggy. His lips twisted into a dry smile. It was a wonder she did not go around bleating like a sheep considering the amount of mutton she must have consumed over the years.

'Howdy Miss Dorothy, good service?' Ben greeted her, as he had done last Sunday.

'A fine service, Mr Crow,' she responded, as she had done last Sunday.

'Leave the horse and buggy to me.'

'With pleasure, Mr Crow.'

He and Miss Dorothy said little to each other, polite chit-chat, no more than that.

The barn door creaked as he led the horse inside.

'I'd best oil that door.' Unlike last Sunday she had followed him into the barn. The door creaked once again as she pushed it closed behind them.

Turning round, Ben saw that she was unbuttoning the front of her gown. Hell, the minister was wrong. The poor unfortunate woman was far from recovered. Her mind still remained addled and he doubted whether she knew what she was doing.

He backed away. 'Now, Miss Dorothy, why don't you go on into the house and fix me some mutton and fried eggs,' he suggested.

'You're a handsome man, Ben Crow, now that you've shaved away your stubble,' she told him.

'Well, I ain't the respectable sort, Miss Dorothy; I ain't your sort.' He'd

31

have to get out of the barn and make a run for it. 'I'm an unbeliever, an immoral gambler.'

She sighed. 'If only things had been different, Mr Crow,' she observed, sounding quite sane. But then she screamed, a high-pitched whistling sound which made Ben think of a train whistle. To Ben's dismay she began to rip at her clothes ferociously, splitting material and scratching at her exposed flesh.

Ben's eyes, however, were not upon Miss Dorothy's flesh. His gaze had fallen upon the pitchfork near the barn door. If she were to take it into her sick mind to snatch up that pitchfork and endeavour to spear him with it, well, he'd heard crazy folk were endowed with awesome strength. He balked at having to restrain Miss Dorothy, but he knew he would have to do it for her own safety and his.

And then, screeching, she launched herself at him, thankfully without the pitchfork. Ben found himself rolling upon the ground as he endeavoured to pinion her arms as she endeavoured to scratch his face.

Next thing he knew the door of the barn burst open allowing sunlight to invade the darkness of the barn. A shaft of sunlight hit himself and Miss Dorothy as they continued to struggle, but she was screeching now, words begging the Lord to help her.

Hands grabbed at Ben tearing him away from the frantically wriggling woman.

'You no-good bastard, Ben Crow,' a hoarse voice, recognizable as the voice of Meaks yelled, as Ben was poleaxed by Meaks's clenched fist. 'I knew you'd try something like this. I just knew it.'

Stunned by the blow, Ben lay on the floor as hard-toed boots thudded into him. If they kept up they'd stomp him to death.

'Now, now, ma'am you come on outside,' a voice soothed. Ben recognized the voice as belonging to Edward Bacon.

'Thank the Lord, Mr Bacon,' she sniffled, 'for He sent you to save me.'

'Miss Dorothy, did that bastard Crow . . .'

A loud wail greeted the question.

'For the sake of decency, boss . . .' Meaks yelled.

'I apologize, Miss Dorothy. You come along now.' The sobs receded as she was led out.

Blackness rushed to envelop Ben. His last thought was that Miss Dorothy was indeed as sane as himself. And she had outsmarted him as only a conniving woman could do.

A bucket of cold water brought Ben round. Consciousness returned slowly, his body awash with pain, protesting as it was brought back from merciful unconsciousness to face harsh reality. And harsh reality was that he lay upon his back, outside now for they must have hauled him out, with his hands tightly lashed behind his back. Once again the words 'a good day to die' filled his head, and if the faces staring down at him were anything to go by then this day would prove to be his last.

Edward Bacon was smiling, Ben saw. Meaks was enraged, as if he were carrying a torch for Miss Dorothy. She'd set him up.

'One word, Crow, and I'll kick the stuffing out of you,' Meaks promised. 'Why'd you ruin Miss Dorothy? There are plenty of no-account women at the Buffalo Head only too willing to oblige,' Meaks continued.

Ben struggled to his feet. His ribs must be cracked; pain lanced through him. But cracked ribs would be the least of his worries for he'd seen the rope hanging from the old cottonwood tree.

'You've bought it, Bacon,' he croaked. 'You've bought the land from Miss Dorothy.'

A blow from Meaks felled Ben.

'Ain't no way that poor shamed woman could be expected to stay in

Mallory,' Bacon replied, with evident self satisfaction. 'Buying her land was the least I could do. And seeing that in the event of your demise the land reverts to Miss Dorothy . . . ' He laughed. 'You ain't dead yet, Crow, but your demise is a mere formality. Every man here can bear witness to your guilt, ain't no point wasting time. It's got to be done so it had best be done now.'

Damn Miss Dorothy and her twisted mind, Ben thought. He had never suspected her true feelings on this matter. He guessed she hadn't the stomach to stay around and see the deed done. No, she'd forked it out pretty damn quick. Bacon must have come here with the Bill of Sale and ready cash. It had never occurred to Ben that a woman would be instrumental in his downfall.

Even though there was no hope, he found himself marking the faces of the men who surrounded him. He'd remember each and every one of them.

Some looked away, for his thoughts were plain.

'Any last words, Crow?' Bacon mocked.

Ben shrugged. No point in uttering threats he could not live up to. He smiled at the thought.

Very slowly, Ben began to walk towards the hanging tree. They'd even brought out a chair from the kitchen, one which he'd sat on many times. Bacon had fixed it so there would be no clean drop, no abruptly snapped neck; Ben Crow was destined to choke slowly to death, his boots a mere foot or so from the ground.

There was silence now. They were waiting for him to break he realized, even hoping for it, especially Bacon and Meaks. Meaks hated him for what he imagined Ben had done to Miss Dorothy and Bacon was just a no-account, sadistic bastard. Face expressionless, Ben climbed upon the chair.

Leastways, Crow, you know how to

die like a man,' a voice grudgingly conceded.

Bacon, eyes glinting, dropped the noose over Ben's neck. Ben felt the hemp rough against his skin. Given a choice he would have opted for a bullet, any man would.

'Damn bastard,' Meaks's control broke, as viciously he kicked the chair from beneath Ben Crow.

★ ★ ★

Ex-lawman Jubal Strike stared down at the scene below in disbelief. Although he no longer wore a badge, Strike felt compelled to intervene. Sighting his telescopic rifle, a gift from an English gent whose life Jubal had saved, the darn fool having got himself lost and all Jubal had done was happen along, Jubal squeezed the trigger. He did not miss.

★ ★ ★

The old man's murder had driven Miss Dorothy crazy. She'd come to Bacon babbling about how her grandpa's spirit haunted the ranch and how she must get away or else she would go mad. She had then stated her proposal, a scheme Bacon himself would not have thought up in a million years.

With genuine pleasure, Bacon watched as Crow, or Crowther or whatever he called himself, rope danced. Crow's face was by now contorted. To Bacon's anger Crow had remained resolute and contemptuous to the last. A hard man Crow, Bacon could not but help acknowledge, and there had been such a consuming hatred in Crow's blue eyes as the noose had fallen about his neck.

'Look out, boss!' Meaks yelled, alerted by the glint of light from the low hill overlooking the spread. The betraying glint had been enough to draw the ramrod's attention from Crow to the hill and the lone rider silhouetted against the skyline.

Even as Meaks yelled his warning, the sound of a rifle overlapped it. Crow dropped to the ground.

'Hell!' Dan, a young waddy, yelled seemingly unaware of his own danger. 'He's shot the damn rope clean through.'

'You damn fools, he's using one of those new-fangled long-distance shooters,' Meaks yelled. 'We haven't a hope in hell. He can pick us off like sitting ducks.'

Strike did not want to be drawn into whatever was going on below for lawbreakers were no longer his concern. Nor did he wish to make them his concern. No, he aimed to stay out of trouble until he had run down Miss Agatha Keeley. He had promised Aggie's long-suffering pa that he would ascertain whether Aggie was in need of help, it being understood that Jubal would supply that help.

'You bring her home hog tied if necessary,' Dan Keeley had said, a tear glinting in his eye.

Sighting his rifle again, Jubal took aim at the white stetson worn by the man he took to be the boss. He aimed to drive them off pretty damn quick. Strike squeezed the trigger.

Bacon's hat went flying. It was warning enough for him. With a yell, he dug in his spurs as a third bullet whistled by. The lynching party took flight, it not occurring to them that whoever was up there was shooting to miss.

Grinning, Jubal descended to lower ground. Nevertheless he kept a wary eye and his rifle at the ready just in case this little confrontation was not concluded.

The sheepherder had been beaten Jubal saw, concluding that folk hereabouts must hate sheep men powerful bad. Oddly, the lynched man's hands were not roughed by honest toil, although there were signs that he'd been working. Frowning, Jubal checked for the pulse he did not expect to find. Something about this did not sit right.

'Hell!' Such was Jubal's haste to cut away the noose his blade nicked the man's skin. Thinning his lips, having no liking for the necessity, Jubal forced himself to breathe air into the lynched man's mouth whilst he pounded away at the man's chest. Jubal had seen this done once and he had seen it work.

There was the chance that the unfortunate herder might revive in body but not in mind. In that event, Jubal guessed he must do his duty and put the unfortunate *hombre* out of his misery. Also, if the herder pulled through, he would not have much of a voice left. Those damned bastards hadn't even afforded the unfortunate *hombre* the mercy of a clean break.

Doggedly Strike worked on.

# 3

'I believe you,' Strike, after due consideration, rejoined. 'You've had a bum deal, Crow.' He paused. 'I know more than most how devious a female mind can be.' He shrugged. 'But the fact is, Crow, it's your word against hers. I'll sign a statement as to what I've witnessed here, but whether the local law will charge Bacon with attempted murder, well . . . '

'It won't,' Ben rasped painfully, his voice so low Strike could hardly hear the words. Ben shrugged; clearly Larkin, the lawman, was in Bacon's pocket, must be for Bacon to believe he could lynch a man with impunity.

Strike didn't waste words on Miss Dorothy. He doubted whether the woman could be prevailed upon to tell the truth. In other words, Crow was out on a limb for Bacon was free to accuse Crow of rape.

'As you ain't deceased, that Bill of Sale is invalid,' Strike mused, 'but if you show your face in town it's you that's liable for arrest, the law being upheld by jackasses from time to time. It sticks in my craw to see a man get away with murder; I'd bet my boots Bacon killed old Sam Church.'

'Maybe you'd lose your boots,' Ben replied with a shrug.

'Huh?' For a moment Strike failed to understand. When understanding dawned, Strike's expression was something to behold. In different circumstances Ben might have laughed. 'You ain't implying Miss Dorothy stove in her grandpa's head . . . ?'

'Maybe,' Ben spoke but the one word. There was no need for further palaver. Not grief but rage had driven Miss Dorothy loco. Rage that she'd been disinherited. And maybe rage that her stubborn miserly mule of a grandpa wouldn't sell out had driven Miss Dorothy to take up a rock and bring it down with considerable force. Rage was a powerful emotion. Ben stood impassive, but he himself was consumed with rage. Most of it directed at Bacon. He'd vowed to kill Bacon by whatever means possible. Bacon did not know it but he was a dead man walking. And maybe Meaks. The crew he would ignore lest they crossed him.

'Any suggestions, Strike?' Ben asked. Had he been able to inject expression into his shattered voice it would have been heavy with sarcasm. To his surprise ex-US Marshal Strike appeared to be considering the question.

'You're in one hell of a mess,' Strike finally rejoined ponderously. 'The odds are against you.' He rubbed his chin. 'Move out, I'd say. Start over with a fresh slate.' He held up a hand as Ben attempted to speak. 'There's a body in the barn. An old Mexican dead of a heart attack I'd say. Maybe seeing you dancing made him think he'd be next.'

'The hired help.' Ben had forgotten

entirely about the old man.

'We can bury him instead of you. Put your marker on his grave. As far as Bacon is concerned you're planted. There'll be no warrant out for you accusing you of violating Miss Dorothy. Think about it, Crow. I'll gamble Bacon will not dig deep to verify the truth. If ex-Marshal Jubal Strike says Ben Crow has been planted deep that's the end of it. Unless you suddenly reappear.'

'I won't!' To hell with the ranch, Ben thought. He was no sheepman. The whole town would side with Bacon, and Miss Dorothy, for she'd been born in Mallory and lived her entire life there, a much-respected woman of good character. Whereas he, Ben Crow, was a no-account gambling man, a rolling stone, just the kind of man to violate Miss Dorothy, so they would say.

'Pack your supplies and get out of here Crow, pronto,' Strike advised, 'for I reckon they'll be back; if not all of them, one at least. Whoever rides in will find me standing beside a freshly dug grave, Good Book in hand.'

'I'm obliged.' Ben turned away. In that moment he had arrived at a decision. Miss Dorothy was not getting away with it. No way. Not that he planned to kill her but sure as hell he'd relieve her of her 'blood money'. He'd hit her where it would hurt the most and that meant her purse. And just maybe allow her to believe that he intended to blast her. What a sight that would make, Miss Dorothy on her knees. Perhaps he'd even make her lick his boots. It was no more than her just deserts for she had conspired to murder him.

Ben rode away. He did not glance back. Damn Miss Dorothy and her apple pies, he thought. And he wished he could forget that particular kind of smile she had given him from time to time. Despite being as scrawny as a broomstick he'd found himself

47

oddly drawn towards old Sam's granddaughter. And wasn't that the darnedest thing, for all she'd wanted was to see him dead?

* * *

Jubal Strike attacked the ground with vigour. He knew Edward Bacon would not live long to enjoy his newly acquired land. There'd been that look in Crow's cold blue eyes which had said more than words. Sweat dotted Strike's faded shirt. He dug deep and rolled the body of the Mexican into the grave. He'd keep his word. He'd say the prayers which needed to be said before riding on. The grave was just halfway filled when Strike saw the approaching riders. Not particularly concerned, Strike leaned on his shovel. Having acquired the old man's land Strike did not believe the rancher would want to complicate matters with an unnecessary killing.

Edward Bacon stared long and hard

at the shorter, sturdily built man. Hard eyes stared back at him.

'Ex-Marshal Jubal Strike,' the stranger introduced himself and then added, 'Mind telling me what the hell is going on? This is your work, ain't it?'

'He's dead!' Meaks stated the obvious.

'A few minutes earlier I'd have saved him,' Strike shrugged. 'I'm waiting.'

Edward Bacon, after introducing himself, was quick to oblige. Had Strike not known differently he might have believed the rancher. Edward Bacon was a plausible sounding man. And clearly the crew did believe Crow had violated Miss Dorothy. Certainly the ramrod Meaks believed it.

'Damn polecat,' Strike rejoined, sourly shovelling further earth into the grave. 'Nevertheless,' he continued, 'I'd be obliged if you'd dismount, Mr Bacon.'

'What the hell for?' Bacon demanded.

'I aim to read from the Good Book,' Strike replied mirthlessly. 'And I'd be obliged if you men would remove your hats whilst I pray for a man meeting his Maker.'

Bacon's relief was laughable. 'Well, I can't argue with that, Marshal Strike.' He paused. 'Are you staying in Mallory?' Bacon's teeth were showing as the man smiled, but Strike wasn't fooled.

'Nope,' he rejoined. 'I'll be making my report and riding out. I've an urgent matter needing my attention. As to whether you face charges, Mr Bacon, I guess that lies with the local law. Even a polecat such as Crow deserves a trial. This hanging was unlawful, Mr Bacon. Ain't no amount of words going to make it right.' Suddenly Strike grinned. 'But rest assured what happens in Mallory ain't my concern.'

* * *

Miss Dorothy believed her fellow passenger was connected to the railroad. Her thin nostrils pinched with distaste. Clearly the man was a glutton as his size testified. He had also been imbibing. The stage stank of stale whiskey. And he stank. But the discomfort was as nothing to her as every moment which passed took her further away from Mallory.

Undoubtedly Edward Bacon was a coward. It had been her hope that Bacon, desperate for Grandpa's land, would simply challenge Mr Crow, provoke him into an outright confrontation upon Main Street. When it became clear that this was not going to happen, her despair had spiralled. Fearing that he might be bested, outdrawn, Bacon feared to challenge Ben Crow.

If only dear Grandpa had listened. She visualized the pink scalp beneath the wispy white hair. She'd crept up on him and picked up a jagged, sharp edged stone and brought it down with all her might. Having struck him once she'd been unable to stop until aching arms had forced her to desist. She had burnt her garments, of course, and taken a cold bath.

Miss Dorothy sighed. Ben Crow had been so good-looking and such a gentleman. But it was not her fault. She had been driven to get rid of him; for clearly the foolish man had a liking for sheep farming. Hadn't he helped old Pedro with the chores. She frowned; she had not seen old Pedro when Bacon had ridden in. Clearly, the old man had made himself scarce.

Miss Dorothy's reflections were abruptly interrupted by loud curses and disgusting profanities from their driver. These were followed by hoots and shots as the stage began to pick up speed lurching from side to side alarmingly.

She found herself thrown against the large belly of the railroad man. He thrust her from him without ceremony as he began to babble his prayers. It was then the awful reality dawned upon her: desperadoes were in pursuit of the stage.

As a girl, she had dreamt of being

carried away by a handsome outlaw, but now Miss Dorothy also began to pray. If only she were back in her kitchen baking an apple pie for Mr Crow . . .

★ ★ ★

Having taken his leave of Jubal Strike, Ben headed towards Mallory. It was his intention to detour around the town, pick up the stage trail and follow on until he caught up with Miss Dorothy. It might take days, weeks, months or years, but Ben did not give a damn.

She'd set him for a lynching party, left him to strangulate real slow at the end of a rope whilst his eyes popped out of his head and red lights flashed before them.

It was not his intention to kill her, or even lay a violent hand upon her, it was enough that she would believe that was his intention. He would have her howling for mercy only too glad to pen her confession and clear his name.

But the thought nagged away at him that Miss Dorothy would not break. She would not pen a confession. With Miss Dorothy clearly being loco nothing could be counted upon.

Ben detoured Mallory, travelling on at a steady pace. He saw no one. He might have been the last man left upon earth and that would have suited him fine. The land in this neck of the woods was mostly flat, dotted with shrubs and with distant hills over-looking the plain. Ben detoured the patches of mesquite with their gnarled black trunks and leaves Ben had often thought of as delicate. Not that he would have voiced such a fanciful thought. Being originally an Easterner he guessed he paid more attention to the scenery than those born and bred on the frontier.

Here and there he spotted a *Palo Verde* which was a damn fool name for a tree. Today, however, he was not in the mood to appreciate the scenery, spectacular though it was.

Miss Dorothy had become the focus of his existence. Bested by a woman, he kept thinking. Fooled by her apple pies. Why had he not suspected that inside she was seething with anger at having been cheated out of her inheritance? And cheated she had been no matter the good intentions of old Sam Church. At least Ben assumed the old Bible thumper had harboured good intentions.

To the left of the trail he heard the warning rattle of a snake. Miss Dorothy hadn't even given a warning rattle before she had struck.

Thinning his lips, Ben rode on. He had skinned and eaten snake before now and had been glad of it. There had been more than one occasion when Ben Crow had been forced to flee town pretty damn quick.

He decided to rest up some at the relay station, drink coffee, chew the cud and maybe discover whether Miss Dorothy might have been so foolish as to discuss her ultimate destination. He thought not. But there was always the chance the woman might unintentionally have let slip a clue — assuming she'd formulated any plans, maybe she hadn't thought beyond getting the cash and getting away from Mallory.

Wisps of thin grey smoke spiralled from the chimney of the relay house, quickly dissipating. A few chickens scratched around in the dirt before the open door of the building. Whoever ran the relay station kept a hog, it being common practice to fatten at least one piglet. The stench from the hog pen was overwhelming. A cloud of fat black flies hovered over the pen dispersing at Ben's approach and then reforming.

The hair on his neck began to prickle. He removed his hat, useful when it came to batting away buzzing bluebottles and cautiously approached the hog pen. He peered over the wooden wall and the sight which greeted him caused him instinctively to step back a pace. Being a man of strong constitution he was able to keep down his meal of fried cornmeal consumed earlier. He didn't curse, albeit he had been ill prepared for the sight which greeted him. His throat was too damn sore for him to want to utter a sound.

It had been in his mind, as he had approached the station, that the relay man maybe was inside snoozing, there not being much to do between the arrival and departure of the stage. The reality was different. The unfortunate *hombre*, or what was left of him, lay face downwards in the filth of the hog pen. The back of his head and been blown away. And if that wasn't enough, the hogs which had, curiously, been left unharmed, clearly ravenous, had been tucking in to human flesh.

If that don't beat all, he thought. Badly shaken, it was his way to make a joke of it. And what a fool he was standing here gawking. He made an excellent target. If he'd had his wits about him he would have ridden in from behind the place and ascertained he was safe. Hell, after his brush with death he wasn't thinking as quick as he ought to. But the man had been dead awhile, so he guessed whoever had done this was gone.

With an assumed nonchalant shrug, Ben jerked open the door of the hog pen. He'd grant the hogs a stay of execution! Damnit he ought to have noticed there were no team horses resting up in the corral. One reason why the place was strangely quiet.

Colt .45 unholstered, Ben approached the house. Inside there was no sign of any disturbance. The long wooden tables, however, remained laden with used dishes, each one scraped clean. Ben saw it clearly. The stage party had fed and departed. The relay man had scraped the plates and had taken the scraps out to the hogs. This had happened presumably once the stage was out of hearing distance. Otherwise they would have heard the shot.

Ben's stomach lurched, the thought

occurring to him that whoever had done this could be in pursuit of the stage. Miss Dorothy might be dead! And goodbye to any confession! Not to mention the wad of bills she was carrying. Cash, Ben considered to be his.

Feeling a skunk, Ben systematically searched the relay station. Whatever had happened to Miss Dorothy had already occurred. He could not prevent it. He pocketed the few dollars he found in a coat hanging behind the door. He also found a box of cigars and half a bottle of whiskey. He filled a couple of empty gunny sacks with supplies. More importantly there was a plentiful supply of slugs. He guessed he would need them and the old-style buffalo gun hanging over the mantel.

His scavenging concluded, Ben killed a chicken, roasted it and ate the bird together with a hunk of rock-hard bread. Swallowing was extremely difficult. Use made his throat feel as though it were being rasped. As chewed,

Ben reflected upon all the unpleasant methods he could use to kill Bacon. Idle thoughts. Bacon would escape lightly with a slug through the head or heart. A liking for cruelty had never been part of Ben's nature.

A conscience he had not known he possessed, surfaced and urged him to do the decent thing and bury the *hombre* out in the pen. Common sense told him he'd wear himself to a frazzle attacking the sun-baked earth. He needed to conserve his strength. Common sense won out. However, as he rode out he stopped by the hog pen — the hogs had mercifully departed — mouthed a silent prayer and then rode out praying that he was wrong in assuming the desperadoes were after the stage. He wasn't much at reading signs, but the numerous droppings he'd noted around the horse trough suggested that more than one had dropped by.

He did not regret the time passed at the relay station. His horse had needed resting and watering. Another man might have ridden the animal into the ground in his haste to catch up with the stage. Dry bones bore testimony to such foolishness.

Circling black specks against a clear blue cloudless sky confirmed his suspicions. Death lay ahead. The stage had been robbed, but murder had been done also. And somehow Ben wasn't surprised. A twisted mind had worked out the ravenous hogs would have started on their former owner. That was why the hogs hadn't been blasted!

The stage lay on its side. The driver and guard lay some distance from the vehicle, evidently having been thrown clear as the vehicle went over. The buzzards had already started on the two dead men. Deliberately Ben averted his gaze. But the horses, although in a pitiful state, still lived. It was their threshing which was keeping the buzzards at bay. The bastard responsible had not troubled to despatch the injured horseflesh, he'd just left them to rot beneath the sun. Drawing his gun, Ben put the horses out of their misery, his shots reverberating in the stillness.

Only then did he clamber upon the overturned stage. In his heart he knew he would discover Miss Dorothy dead inside. It was gloomy within the stage and a tornado of flies expressed their resentment at Ben's intrusion.

'Damn bastards,' he croaked painfully, waving his hat frantically. He was overwhelmed with relief. There was but the one body and that did not belong to Miss Dorothy. Her fellow passenger had been a portly middle-aged man.

Hell! The bastards must have taken Miss Dorothy along with them. True they might dispose of her along the way having had their fun, but they might not. There was no doubt in his mind. His original intention had been to run Miss Dorothy down. And run her down he would, whether she be dead or alive. It went without saying if she were alive these desperadoes wouldn't hand her over along with her ill-gotten gains.

Which meant he'd have to kill them. Every last one.

Having thus decided, Ben gripped the corpse beneath the armpits and proceeded to haul the dead man out. Considerably outweighed, Ben lost his balance, fell backwards and went down upon the ground, the putrefying corpse on top of him. He rolled free. And swore.

The passenger had not died of a broken neck or even a bullet; this killing had been given a personal touch. Ben could clearly visualize the scene: the terrified, shaken passenger clambering from the stage ready to beg for his life. Whoever had been up top had let the fat man get his head and shoulders out and had then slipped a strand of thin wire around that portly neck before proceeding to garrotte him.

Sure as hell Ben knew what he might expect should he be so unfortunate as to fall into the clutches of this particular *hombre*. This man beat Edward Bacon hands down. Bacon did not even come close. Bacon's motivation for wrongdoing was greed; perversity drove this other.

But it made not a mite of difference. Miss Dorothy and her blood money was what Ben wanted. And that was what he aimed to get. He'd follow that woman to Hell if necessary.

As he rode out, Ben had a hunch that Hell might just lie ahead!

# 4

Ben made slow progress. But there was nothing he could do about it; his forte was dealing the deck; tracking was something else. Whoever he was after drew steadily ahead each hour that passed.

It was his expectation to find Miss Dorothy dead upon the trail ahead. She'd be slowing them down and they'd soon tire of having her along. Having had their fun they'd most likely slit her throat or shoot her.

Dark circling specks appeared to confirm his expectations. It was midday now and the sun was hot. Ben saw that he had arrived at the place they had made night camp. But the body, lying by the ashes of the long dead fire, to his relief and disbelief did not belong to Miss Dorothy. It was a man, or what remained of him who lay dead.

Someone had stuck a knife in his side. Neither had that knife been retrieved. It had been left where it had been thrust.

'Goddamnit!' Ben croaked painfully. He recognized the white-handled knife. There had been a pair of them in Miss Dorothy's kitchen. Her chopping knives. Ben didn't doubt it: it had to be Miss Dorothy who had knifed the man.

He studied the scuffed ground. There'd been one hell of a struggle. And Miss Dorothy, who'd brought along her kitchen knives when she'd fled the sheep ranch, had managed to get one out of her pocket. And then she had let her tormentor have it. Forcibly. Straight into the side puncturing vital organs.

Obviously the galoot had done or was trying to do what Miss Dorothy had falsely accused Ben himself of doing. Ben, despite what she'd done to him, could not help feel pity for Miss Dorothy and her predicament. He could not bring himself to think about what might be done to Miss Dorothy now, by way of retaliation.

He was no knight in shining armour. Miss Dorothy was not a princess and it was too damn late to save her from her fate, but Ben knew he could not turn back. He and this loco killer were on collision course. What he'd have to do now was try and put himself in the other man's boots. He'd have to try and think the way this bastard thought. But he had a hunch it might not be possible. The twisted galoot plainly didn't think like anyone Ben had ever encountered.

Expression sombre, Ben resumed his pursuit.

★ ★ ★

Mexico hadn't changed. Thinning his lips, Ben regarded the basking gila monster. Three feet long, black, venomous and deadly.

The galoot he was pursuing wouldn't

be three feet long nor black, but sure as hell he was venomous and deadly. Further evidence of the galoot's perverse inclinations had been discovered by Ben only yesterday. Ben knew all kinds of men, men who killed just for the hell of it, cold-blooded, detached killers such as Linelli who killed for cash, but never before had he run across a galoot who found his pleasure in roasting folk.

The man, or what was left of him, found by Ben on the trail, had been torched. A stake had been set in rock-hard earth — they'd actually taken time to dig earth and to collect dry brush — then the unlucky wayfarer had been bound to the stake, brush piled presumably around his lower legs and torched.

Ben reckoned the man had died hard and had been a long time dying. It did not take much imagination to envisage the *hombre* dying slow, piece by piece, as his flesh blistered before finally peeling away.

So affected by his grisly discovery had Ben been that he'd vomited his breakfast of prairie chicken.

At first, as he had approached the pitiful remains, he had feared that he would discover they belonged to Miss Dorothy, which was entirely reasonable considering she'd driven her kitchen knife into one of the galoot's men.

Burying what was left, Ben had decided that the perverse bastard would have forced poor old Dorothy to watch the torture. That would be a way of hurting her real bad. It didn't take much to drive a woman over the edge, or so Ben considered. The isolation most endured laid the foundations, the death of a child could do the rest, or watching a man melt and bubble, being forced to listen to the agonizing screams.

Hell, despite what the she-devil had done to him he was feeling sorry for her again. Which proved he was a damn fool, leastways where women were concerned.

The gila monster blinked, but apart from that did not move. Ben considered that it was lucky for the reptile that it was he, Ben Crow, regarding it and not that crazy fiend from Hell.

It figured that the galoot would choose to hole up in Mexico. Here, across the border, the pursuit of justice was lax enough. Everyone could be bribed. Also Ben figured that the peons living in this area would know of such a man.

Shading his eyes, Ben squinted at the towering, still distant rocks. He'd be up there, amongst them. Ben decided he'd call the man Escorpión. Escorpión was as good a sobriquet as any. And well deserved.

Even Escorpión would have to buy supplies just like normal folk. So it figured the village where Escorpión went shopping for his supplies was not in danger of being razed. Escorpión's men would want a cantina in which to drink themselves stupid and buy the company of whores. Escorpión's village. Find that and he would find Escorpión.

Head up into the hills and he might never find him. Worse, Escorpión might find him first. Recalling the torched remains, Ben's stomach heaved. Go after him and there was a chance that he himself might share that man's fate.

Ben had a hunch Escorpión had torched a total stranger. Just for the hell of it. Because he liked to do it. The thought came into his mind then, that maybe he'd been spared for a purpose: to rid the world of Escorpión. This deed was no mean feat. He smiled grimly. He was walking on egg shells; a wrong decision would be sure to mean death and an unpleasant one at that. So what next, he asked himself?

Due east of here was the garrison town of San Paulo. Linelli had been held in the town's fortress prison. Suddenly Ben thought of the garrison's commander, that skunk De Bois. Hell, he ought to have thought of De Bois sooner. If anyone would know what the hell was going on hereabouts it would be De Bois. The cunning commander had ears all over the place.

But would De Bois be prepared to talk? Talking of Escorpión could bring down his wrath, but as a fort commander, De Bois ought to be safe enough. Ben fingered the handle of his knife. He did not have money with which to bribe De Bois so if necessary he must resort to other means. He would do what had to be done and if De Bois knew anything, before Ben was finished he'd know it too.

He dug in his heels confident that he had made the right decision. Before he could even think of saving Miss Dorothy he needed to know who it was he was going after.

* * *

De Bois, highly polished boots resting upon his desk, watched as a bloated brown bug disappeared into one of the numerous cracks in the walls. The

72

garrison was infested with them. Idly, De Bois wondered if wiping over the walls with kerosene would eliminate the bugs. He'd drawn the short straw when he'd been assigned to this bug hole, but he was making the best of a bad lot.

If anyone in authority had cared to examine the garrison's records, certain anomalies would have come to light. Under De Bois's stewardship, a good many prisoners had either 'died' whilst incarcerated or escaped.

Linelli had fetched the highest price. De Bois found it hard to understand how anyone could look upon that cold-blooded killer as a pard, but the gambler Ben Crow had been willing to shell out plenty to save Linelli's hide.

Crow, De Bois sensed, was a true gentleman such as himself. Linelli, of course, was scum. As was Gonzalez! Gonzalez, who presumed to think that he, Franco De Bois, would want to wed his fat, unattractive daughter.

With a clatter, his boots dropped to the floor. He cast one last look at his reflection and was pleased with what he saw. Even visiting the whores of San Paulo he took the trouble to dress finely, as befitted a gentleman. He was a handsome man he knew, and the ladies seemed to like his clean-shaven look and shoulder-length brown hair.

For tonight's outing, he had chosen to wear a black satin jacket, white ruffled shirt and red satin waistcoat; tight, side-braided trousers completed the picture.

In the dung heap that was San Paulo, money could buy just about anything and when it came to satisfying his pleasures the whores of this town had proved very accommodating. When he was eventually recalled to Mexico City he would take away with him certain memories. He smiled; if anyone could make the best of a bum deal it was himself.

The last time he had been in San Paulo, Ben's circumstances had been vastly different. For one thing he had not stunk like a skunk. He'd been decently dressed in a black, pin-striped suit and clean white shirt and there had been gold cuff links at his wrists. Now he was just another no-account, stinking bum on his way through with scarcely the funds to buy himself a shot of cheap whiskey.

He had in fact foregone the whiskey choosing to put his horse in stabling and have his boots mended. He'd also restocked his gunny sacks with the basic provisions, his remaining money going on shells.

When he grabbed De Bois it was his intention to help himself to whatever change De Bois might have left over after taking his pleasure. The last time he'd been here, Ben himself had been the target of many a hard-eyed female on the prowl; this time not one of them spared him a glance. When he moved out, no one in San Paulo would even remember he'd been here, which suited him just fine.

Since arriving in San Paulo, Ben had spent his nights in a particular part of the town, the part he knew De Bois liked to frequent. Whilst reconnoitring Ben had learnt a good deal about De Bois. In fact, to get Linelli out, Ben had hit upon the idea of jumping De Bois one dark night, taking him back to the fort knife pressed against his side and forcing De Bois to release Linelli along with two fast horses. No matter that the plan was flawed it had been all that Ben had been able to come up with.

And then the suave, conceited De Bois had approached him hinting in a roundabout way Linelli could walk free for a price. As the younger son, De Bois had confided, he had found himself, through no fault of his own, impoverished.

Ben had taken a gamble De Bois had done this before. He'd also gambled De Bois would keep his word, if only because killing the escapee would scupper any future plans De Bois might have.

So now Ben sat, back against a

wall, in an alleyway practically on top of a stinking pile of garbage yet to be cleared. Rustling sounds in the darkness suggested to Ben that rats were at the garbage. After eight days of vigil Ben had become accustomed to the stink and the rustling.

Sometimes Ben whiled away the time thinking how it would be to amuse himself with the fastidious Miss Dorothy, the cause of his downfall. He'd never do it, but it was good to think about it whilst he waited for De Bois to feel the urge to indulge himself. That was when he intended to grab De Bois, after he'd taken his pleasure, when his guard was down. Hell, he would like to be a fly on the wall when De Bois got started for De Bois liked working as a threesome. But it was too risky putting an eye to the shutters, there being a good chance someone would try to stick a knife into his back; even saddle-tramps weren't safe from would-be robbers.

Peering from the shadows, Ben saw

the shape of a horseman and smelt the strong, overpowering scent that De Bois favoured.

'About time you bastard, about time,' Ben muttered, feeling he'd never rid himself of the stench of the garbage.

De Bois dismounted, spurs jingling, and then stopped to light a match. Ben caught a glimpse of pinched nostrils as De Bois breathed in the fetid stench of decay. Then De Bois, cigar lit, disappeared into the simple white stone dwelling.

Ben knew there were two women within. He listened to the high-pitched giggles and other sounds which sounded interesting. De Bois took his time. A rat ran over Ben's foot. He almost let out a yell himself at that.

Finally, De Bois stepped out, adjusted his jacket and looked around for his horse. With a curse, De Bois started picking his way up the rutted street intent on finding the straying animal.

An overwhelming stench washed over De Bois as a wiry arm clamped itself around his windpipe. He did not struggle, feeling the hard muzzle of a gun pressed against his spine as he was pulled backwards into the alleyway.

Knowing he had to move quickly, Ben shoved De Bois face downwards upon the garbage pile. A choking sound came from De Bois, a sound not occasioned by Ben's arm which had been removed but by the stench of the garbage.

Planting his knee in the small of De Bois's back, Ben seized the man's long hair, jerking the head upwards, at the same time placing the blade of his knife against De Bois's throat.

'You're going to talk,' he rasped, meaning that De Bois would tell him all that he wished to know, but perhaps misunderstanding, De Bois began to speak, pleading desperately for his life, offering bribes by way of inducement to be spared.

Ben had no choice but to let the fool run out of steam. 'Talk about a galoot who goes round burning folk for the fun of it,' Ben said when De Bois at last fell silent. 'I know you know,' Ben bluffed. 'Why, you might even have a finger in the pie.'

'The mad man,' De Bois wheezed. 'Gonzalez shelters him that is all I know.'

'You know more,' Ben urged. 'Who the hell is this Gonzalez and why does he shelter this lunatic?' By way of inducement Ben shoved De Bois's face deeper into the garbage. He grinned in the darkness. De Bois's fancy duds were done for. No amount of washing would remove the stench and as for De Bois himself, well, now he had a different smell altogether and it would take a powerful lot of soaking and soap before it could be removed.

'The *patron* is mad,' De Bois wheezed again. 'He cut out a man's tongue for . . . for talking . . . '

'I'll keep my lips sealed if that's what is worrying you,' Ben promised.

'True, the man was only a *peon*,' De Bois mused.

'Spill the beans or I'll cut out your entrails,' Ben promised, thinking he'd have to outdo this man called *patron*, old Escorpión.

Believing the threat, De Bois began to talk wildly.

'You stinking vermin,' De Bois concluded, 'I have told you all I know.'

'Yeah, I believe you.' Ben had a hunch De Bois was close to breaking. He still thought having his entrails cut out was a possibility. 'Hell, the only entrails I'm going to cut out will belong to the *patron*,' Ben joshed. 'Now stay put for a while. If I spot you moving whilst I'm riding out I'll take off your head.'

That little speech had strained his throat badly Ben thought, anger flaring inside him. Hell, he might never have a chance to kill Edward Bacon.

He could not turn back. He had to go on. And he must put Bacon out of his thoughts. It was some consolation to think that maybe one day Linelli would drift into Mallory intent upon looking up his old pard Ben Crow.

Ben knew Linelli. When Linelli heard Ben Crow had been lynched, Linelli would go gunning for Bacon. And doubtless Linelli would use worked-upon slugs, the kind that shattered into fragments upon impact. So one could say Bacon was a dead man walking and Meaks, too, if the ramrod was still around.

'I'd advise you not to draw attention to yourself plastered in filth,' Ben mouthed against De Bois's ear. 'You'd never live it down.' That truth alone would be enough to stop De Bois raising the alarm, it would be enough to send De Bois slinking back to the fort intent upon avoiding detection.

★ ★ ★

Meaks crossed into Mexico with Bacon's laughter and derision still fresh in his mind.

'Darn fool!' Bacon had yelled. 'Who

the hell do you think stove in the back of old Sam's skull? Me? Well, think again. And how in tarnation do you think we just happened along and found Crowther . . . ? You dumb bastard, Meaks. You find that female and you'll find trouble. She ain't going to fall into your arms. Why, she's liable to . . .'

What Bacon had said stayed with Meaks. That and the thought he had helped lynch an innocent man. Miss Dorothy had done for Ben Crow. And old Sam. But still Meaks had to know, know what fate had befallen Miss Dorothy.

# 5

Ben left San Paulo deeming it unwise to stay around. After his humiliation, De Bois would be out for blood. Ben made camp a safe distance from the town. What he had learnt had given him plenty to think about. There was a link between the two, the rancher Gonzalez and the man Ben had nicknamed Escorpión.

Ben had discovered that the crazy bastard referred to himself as the Devil's friend. How the hell was he going to save Miss Dorothy from the Devil's friend? That was the thought constantly gnawing away at him, that and the fact he must be crazy himself even to try and save Miss Dorothy after what she'd done to him.

Ben gathered that although Gonzalez did not employ Escorpión, the bandit leader was only too happy to deal with those foolish enough to cross Gonzalez. The ways in which Escorpión dealt with the men Gonzalez wanted removed were unusually savage, a simple slug not being enough for the lunatic.

Rolling his smoke, Ben conceded it would be impossible to get to Escorpión. Escorpión was holed up on hills situated on Gonzalez's range. No doubt the concealed trails leading up to Escorpión's hideaway would be well guarded. Any fool trying to sneak up on Escorpión would very likely be shot down, or worse, taken captive. De Bois, of course, didn't give a damn about the reign of terror by these two men. All De Bois seemed concerned about was the condition of his uniform and the shine of his boots.

Well, the only way forward seemed to be to get Escorpión down out of the mountains. To do that he'd need to stir up a hornets' nest. Yep, he'd have to stir them up and await developments.

They'd know then someone was out to get the pair of them, but they wouldn't know who and they wouldn't know why. Ben knew Escorpión wouldn't connect any of it with his acquisition of Miss Dorothy.

After having spoken with De Bois, Ben knew now what Gonzalez cared most about. Escorpión, of course, cared most about killing folk as unpleasantly as possible, but Gonzalez now had another concern and it was not his fat daughter, the one Gonzalez was keen to see married to De Bois.

Ben settled back on his blanket and, as he lay there looking up at the stars, a sudden understanding came to him. That ugly bastard Meaks had been sweet on Miss Dorothy. That explained the hate he'd seen on Meaks's face. Hell, the last thing he wanted was Meaks blundering into all this. Meaks would be no help, just a damn hindrance.

* * *

Meaks rode away from Mallory burdened by the knowledge that he had assisted in the murder of an innocent man. Crow hadn't laid a finger on Miss Dorothy. That Bacon had hanged an innocent man just to get his hands on a stinking sheep ranch beggered belief. Meaks felt only contempt for his boss. A decent man would have challenged Crow and shot it out man to man. That's what Meaks would have done. Meaks scowled; he guessed the railroad must be coming to Mallory, which would explain Bacon's need to get Miss Dorothy's land.

Well, leastways Miss Dorothy had not been prompted by greed. Just a need to get away from Mallory. Meaks decided Miss Dorothy was highly strung, although he was uncomfortably aware others would have used different words.

As the trail was cold, Meaks decided he would head straight for San Paulo. Maybe he'd speak with the commander of the Mexican garrison. If border raiders were abroad, the man would doubtless be endeavouring to hunt the vermin down. Meaks reckoned all he'd need would be a pointer, a suggestion of where the bandits might be found and he'd do the rest. He'd save Miss Dorothy and, damn it, he'd declare himself.

Thinking of that luckless bastard Ben Crow rotting away in an unmarked grave left a sour taste in his mouth. Maybe if Miss Dorothy repented they could put it behind them. Doggedly Meaks refused to believe she might be dead.

* * *

Smiling unpleasantly, Ben approached the log cabin De Bois had told him about. Whether Miss Dorothy was dead by now, and she might be, well, it didn't have any bearing on this. Ben had decided the two females who lived in that cabin had to be stopped from what they'd been doing — and doing successfully because no one hereabouts dared speak about it.

Ben had discovered that Gonzalez had men tunnelling away below the earth, no better than gophers, save gophers saw the light of day. To cut the cost of keeping the place running Gonzalez used slave labour in his silver mine. He'd been doing it for years, Escorpión being used to hunt down anyone who had managed to escape. There'd been precious few and the unlucky few had met a savage end.

The only amusing thing about all this was that Gonzalez had named his hell-hole the Elena Gonzalez Mine after his fat daughter.

As Ben slowly drew near to the cabin two figures came out of the cabin. He regarded them thoughtfully. He guessed they'd been watching out for him. There was water here. He guessed this spot drew in a good many unwary travellers, border crossers moving in both directions.

It had been with reluctance De Bois

had spilled the beans about these two. Ben guessed it was because De Bois feared Gonzalez might make a connection between De Bois and what was going to happen here. A realist, Ben knew De Bois would be regretting the fact that he had blabbed, he would keep his lips buttoned about that. To do anything else would be to sign his own death warrant, fort commander though he was.

Dismounting, Ben studied the women who now approached him with curiosity. They were grandmother and granddaughter, the old woman having a face like a wrinkled apple. Her mouth was drawn back in a toothless smile of welcome as she hobbled towards him. Ben found it hard to hide his disgust; he knew she was not the harmless old woman she liked to fool folk into believing she was.

The girl was pretty he had to admit. Black hair reached to her waist. Her smile almost fooled him; he could almost believe De Bois must have lied about all this — almost, but not quite for his welcome was a mite too warm. It would have been more natural to have been greeted with two loaded shotguns.

He knocked the dust from his clothes. He still looked a saddle-bum. 'Any chance of some water, ma'am?' he rasped. 'I'll pay well for it.' And indeed many had paid well, with their lives.

'Indeed you will not!' she exclaimed. 'Water is the sky's gift to the earth. Here it is free. If you want to stay tonight we can feed you as well.'

'That's risky, ma'am,' he managed to rejoin with a perfectly straight face, 'inviting a saddle-bum to share your home.'

'Aah, but we can see you are an honourable man.' Her voice took on a note of pity which Ben found irritating. 'You are afflicted?'

'Rope burn, ma'am,' he rasped. He gave a mirthless grin. 'You could say I've been brought back from the dead.' If this didn't beat all, the little Jezebel evincing concern and pity for his condition. 'If you're willing to feed me, I'm willing to eat.' His answer he saw at once pleased them; the two varmints had been afraid he'd take his water and ride on.

He continued to look at the girl. She was certainly pleasing to the eye, a lot more pleasing than sour-faced Miss Dorothy. 'It's been a while since a good-looking woman has cooked for me,' he complimented her suddenly, thinking of Miss Dorothy and her apple pies. This pair were a darn sight worse than Miss Dorothy.

Ben had never considered himself a humorous man, but he guessed the Devil had gotten into him. These two would do anything to keep him here overnight.

'Any chance of a hot tub, ma'am?' he enquired. 'I'm trail weary and worn out.'

They kept grinning at him, but he saw they didn't like the idea. But when the old woman gave an almost imperceptible nod the girl managed to convey it would be no trouble at all.

Ben didn't help with the water that had to be heated and hauled to the tin bath. He sat and watched thinking that in their own way these two were a pair of lesser Escorpións.

By the time she had fixed a blanket to separate the tub from the rest of the room, her smile was beginning to slip a little. Ben placed his Peacemaker on a stool beside the tub, undressed, climbed in and lay back to enjoy the feel of hot water. Behind the blanket he could hear the two whispering. He grinned; while he was here he might as well have them wash his dirty clothes. He guessed the old woman would have that job to do. The girl would be busy emptying out the filthy bath water.

'You are a handsome man,' she said, when he finally reappeared smelling strongly of carbolic soap — an improvement on how he'd smelt previously. He guessed she was admiring his blond hair. It had always seemed to attract the ladies. It was growing some now because he was in need of a barber.

'Thank you, ma'am,' he rejoined respectfully. He wasn't fooled, Miss Dorothy had liked the look of him, but good looks had not swayed Miss Dorothy from her chosen path and they would not sway these two. 'It's a puzzle to me,' he continued innocuously, 'Why Gonzalez allows you two ladies to squat on his land.' That had them worried for a moment he noted with satisfaction.

'The *patron* is a good man,' the old woman muttered.

'Well, I reckon you ladies know best,' Ben agreed. He was enjoying himself. Glancing towards the corner he saw that one of them was actually fixing to bake him an apple pie.

And he ate it, two huge wedges, but he declined the wine they kept inviting him to sample. 'I'm tee-total ladies, can't abide the demon drink,' he lied cheerfully. 'Maybe a pitcher of lemonade, if you've a mind to make it. I've a powerful thirst for I've been eating dust for days.' As he'd expected they were only too pleased to make him a pitcher of lemonade.

Later, as he lay behind the curtain on the straw-stuffed mattress which was his bed, the girl came in with his lemonade. 'My grandmother sleeps,' she whispered. Ben doubted it, but he didn't argue. He didn't reckon he'd look this particular gift horse in the mouth. 'Would you care for some company?' she giggled.

Ben patted the mattress. 'Well, I'd be a fool to say no.' She was doing better than Miss Dorothy; she had never offered to keep him company.

After the girl had left him, Ben poured the lemonade out of the window. He'd done his best and she'd seemed to appreciate his efforts. He kind of hoped she'd have a change of heart. He returned to his mattress and, when he thought it was time, began to snore loudly.

He was aware of the two almost at

once, standing there looking down at him. 'Such a man,' he heard her tell the old woman regretfully.

The old woman tutted with impatience. 'He is a lazy pig, Granddaughter, as all men are,' she replied. 'Go and set the signal.'

Ben didn't hear the girl argue so he guessed his endeavours hadn't been good enough for she'd evidently gone to set the signal. He waited and continued to snore.

The sound of horses outside confirmed what he already knew. They were here, Gonzalez's men, to take a supposedly drugged pilgrim off to work for Gonzalez. Ben guessed they worked the prisoners until they dropped dead.

Silently he crossed to the window. There were two of them, dark shapes, hirelings, enjoying a cigar before they came for him. Damn fools, he thought. Well, he was going to kill these two whose names he would never know. He guessed Gonzalez wouldn't know their names either.

He stood with his back against the wall, facing the curtain, Peacemakers drawn, his fingers light on the triggers. He found the cool butts of his weapons comforting. He put great reliance on his Colt .45. So far his guns had seen him through.

They were coming; the old woman pausing to haggle as she explained that the American was big and strong and would last a long time, so clearly she wanted more money. The haggling concluded, the curtain was roughly jerked down.

Ben shot them both where they stood, staring stupidly at him, the lantern held by one of them casting flickering flames. They dropped like sacks, both shot through the heart. Ben guessed they deserved it for they had done this before, many times.

The air inside the small cabin was acrid with the smell of gunfire. From the way the two women regarded him, he guessed they expected to be gunned down. And then the girl, recovering her wits, moved. She lunged for a rifle leaning against the wall.

Ben moved himself. He struck out, sending her sprawling and grabbed the rifle quickly rendering it useless. They had to get out; already flames occasioned by the broken lamp were beginning to take hold. He grabbed the women, one under each arm and hauled them out of the cabin. However, as soon as he had released the pair the old woman hobbled back towards the cabin. Ben was about to go after her, but something made him turn to face the girl.

Face wild with fury, she hurled a knife at him. Ben managed to throw himself to one side. And then she hurled herself at him, nails clawing for his eyes. Worse than that, she tried to snatch at one of his Peacemakers.

'Hell!' Ben clenched his fist and punched her on the chin.

He knew why the old woman had gone back inside; doubtless they kept their cash box hidden in the cabin, their blood-money, money paid for every unfortunate bastard who'd been hauled away to toil underground for old Gonzalez.

He would have saved the old woman if he could but he guessed it was too risky. They must have had kerosene stored inside. The place was going up like a torch. He heard one terrible scream and then there was a merciful silence.

He stared at the girl. What had occurred between them might never have happened. She sat nursing her jaw, eyes dull. 'My brother,' she gurgled. 'My brother will see you burn.'

'Hell!' Ben stepped back a pace not in fear but in shock. De Bois had not told him all. Maybe De Bois did not know these two were related to Escorpión, the killer's grandmother and sister no less.

Very slowly, without taking his eyes from the girl, Ben backed towards his horse which was penned close at hand. Inexplicably she was actually blaming him for her misfortune quite ignoring the fact that she'd been prepared to consign him to a living hell.

Ben smiled unpleasantly. Before he was through here he'd see Gonzalez' silver mine blown sky high.

★ ★ ★

Gonzalez had been forced to listen to Amigo talking about his new woman, whom he called Miss Dorothy. As Amigo talked, it had begun to dawn upon Gonzalez that Amigo and Miss Dorothy shared a similar trait: they were both deranged. Neither had Miss Dorothy been driven mad by Amigo, quite clearly she was deranged before he'd taken her from the stage.

Why, yesterday night, Amigo continued with admiration, Miss Dorothy had attempted to plunge a knife she'd concealed into his throat. He'd grabbed her wrist as the knife had been descending. He'd been lying feigning sleep awaiting her murderous attack.

Miss Dorothy had not disappointed him.

It was clear to Gonzalez that Amigo was impressed with Miss Dorothy. Wisely, Gonzalez refrained from stating the obvious, that the woman was clearly mad. No doubt the woman's insanity had saved her. Crazy bastard that he was, Amigo had in his time burnt women as well as men.

Gonzalez tried not to stare at Amigo's snake eyes. One of them was black, for during the struggle, Miss Dorothy had punched him in the eye.

'She is a jewel,' Amigo concluded, 'a jewel amongst women.'

'Undoubtedly,' Gonzalez wisely agreed. 'And what of your other woman?'

'I have handed her over to my men.'

Which was a pity, Gonzalez thought for he'd had his eye on the girl. Amigo would have known it. If only he did not need Amigo how different things might be. He might kill Amigo.

'She has killed twice this woman,' Amigo confided. 'Three times if we count Pancho. Poor Pancho, how could he have known we had such a woman amongst us?' Amigo paused.

'Who did she kill?' Gonzalez feigned interest.

'Her grandfather and a man she calls poor Benjamin. So what brings you to me, my friend?'

'You're to give the burning a rest,' Gonzalez stated without preamble. 'You're drawing attention to yourself and to me. Questions have been asked in Mexico City. And across the border.'

'De Bois!' Amigo essayed.

'Has responded as always. He knows nothing of this, but will mount a search.' Gonzalez downed a brandy. 'Just amuse yourself with this Miss Dorothy, will you?'

Amigo smiled. 'I am a nobody. And I have your protection as is my right.'

'Look at it this way.' Gonzalez had seen the odd glint in Amigo's eye.

'You're having more fun terrorizing the territory and burning whoever takes your fancy than you would have struggling to keep a ranch running profitably.'

'Not to mention a silver mine,' Amigo laughed unpleasantly.

'Not to mention a silver mine,' Gonzalez agreed uneasily.

'Ah that silver mine. I want my share. My half. Half of the profit every month; half for my sister and I. Maria will go to Mexico City, a great lady and I . . . '

Gonzalez was spared from hearing Amigo's plans, for voices yelled out loudly and with consternation. Amigo did not stir from his seat. He let Gonzalez lift his bulk from the chair and go out to investigate. Amigo merely helped himself to another cigar and then several more which he pocketed.

Gonzalez glared at his fat daughter. 'Get back to your room. This is not your concern.'

Elena didn't argue. She turned and

103

went back upstairs. One day this ranch would belong to Franco De Bois because her father had said she must marry De Bois. But if she didn't marry De Bois and if her father was to die, then this ranch would belong to her, Elena Gonzalez. Shut away in her rooms she had of late been thinking a good deal.

Amigo could envisage himself as a prosperous rancher. There was the daughter, fat Elena, to be removed and Gonzalez must be persuaded to make a new Will but . . . he smiled for he found his thoughts pleasing.

'*Dios*!' Gonzalez exclaimed as he stepped outside. He hardly recognized the dishevelled woman crawling on her hands and knees towards his ranch as Maria, shoeless, with bleeding feet, clothes and body torn by the thorns she had come into contact with during her tortuous journey here.

Who, Gonzalez wondered wildly, who could have been so foolish as to hurt Maria, sister to the madman

Amigo? Truly, Amigo must have made a reckless enemy, another madman, another lunatic, for only a lunatic would have brought Maria to this sorry state. This enemy must be a man who cared nothing for life, for the fool, by his actions, was already a dead man.

Gonzalez did not rush to help Maria. He left that to his fat clucking housekeeper. Nor did it occur to him that Maria's plight might have anything to do with his silver mine, the mine Maria supplied, for a price, with workers.

Maria forced herself to her knees. She gazed wildly at Gonzalez. 'My grandmother,' she croaked, 'dead. Your men, dead!'

Only then, as her words registered, did Gonzalez go to the girl.

# 6

Ben's conscience was bothering him. Of course, the old woman had only herself to blame. He could not have foreseen that the shack was going to burn with her inside; he'd intended to burn the place with the women safely outside, but, nevertheless, he did blame himself. It helped somewhat, however, to remind himself those two had despatched a good many to work for Gonzalez.

He'd left Maria to fend for herself knowing that she'd head straight for Gonzalez. Gonzalez, presumably, being nearer than her crazy brother. When it came to burning, Ben knew that if ever he found himself at her mercy, Maria would cheerfully light the kindling beneath him. Having left Maria, Ben had set course for Gonzalez' mine.

He approached the place under cover

of darkness thinking it fortunate that the gigantic rock formations scattered around Gonzalez' private hell afforded a certain amount of cover. They also helped to conceal the existence of the place. Ben guessed that suited Gonzalez just fine.

As dawn broke, the new day found Ben concealed amongst the acclivities overlooking the mine. He knew he'd have to stay put until darkness returned again. This didn't bother him, for he was a patient and meticulous man.

Daylight revealed that the mine was fortified. Three barbed-wire fences encircled the place. If a man made it over the first fence, then he'd have another two to deal with. Ben did not think it likely that anyone ever made it over the first fence, although on closer inspection he reached the conclusion that a few unlucky souls had escaped.

Unlucky because they'd been hunted down, by Escorpión naturally, hauled back and dealt with. And Ben knew just how they'd been dealt with. There was a metal post set in the middle of the space before the gaping mouth of the mine. Ben knew what it was. The burning stake. There was still charred wood around the stake's base.

Ben watched the luckless *hombres* emerge from the sheds in which they'd been penned for the night. From the look of the ragged workforce, victuals were in short supply. Only when each man reached the mouth of the mine were his shackles removed. He also noted that the guards, hardcases all, were ever watchful, ever vigilant, even though there was little likelihood of any of those miserable wretches choosing to jump a gun-toting guard.

The sun rose in the sky and the earth baked. Ben lay perfectly still, his shirt stained with sweat, his eyes still fixed upon the mine. There were no weaknesses so to speak. Well, maybe one. These guards were intent upon keeping their workers from getting out, maybe night-time they were not so vigilant when it came to stopping a fellow from getting in. A man could sneak into this place under cover of darkness, if he were so minded, if he were loco. Ben guessed that he was, because if he were sane he would not be in Mexico.

Ben found himself wondering what he'd do if Escorpión were to show up here and now. And maybe Gonzalez. The temptation would be to sight his rifle and endeavour to end this business before it got started. Of course, if he missed he'd be in one hell of a mess. However, he had a hunch the two would not be showing up today. Dealing with them was not going to be easy.

★ ★ ★

Gut instinct told Meaks to keep his mouth shut.

The man had ridden openly into Meaks's camp. Very slowly, rifle held casually, Meaks had risen to his feet and faced the stranger. Meaks was

109

ready at any moment to drop to his knee, level, sight his rifle and fire. Not that Meaks was so foolish to think it would be that easy.

Meaks would have bet his last dollar the olive-complexioned *hombre* was a professional killer. The gunbelt had been studded with dollars and that spoke for itself. This man deliberately contrived to draw attention to his gunbelt and the two pearl-handled Colts.

'Got any food to spare, friend?' the other asked softly, cold-brown eyes glinting.

Meaks shrugged. 'You can help yourself to fried chicken and coffee.'

Very slowly and carefully, his unwelcome guest dismounted and approached Meaks's camp-fire. With a rifle in his hand Meaks ought to have the advantage. However, Meaks had an uncomfortable feeling this was not the case.

For a while the gunman was quiet as he gave the fried chicken and coffee his attention. Meaks didn't dare relax. For all he knew the *hombre* might be in desperate need of a stake.

'You have come from Mallory,' the gunman observed without preamble.

For a brief moment Meaks was tempted to lie. But something about his companion killed the lie before it was uttered.

'Yup,' he rejoined, thinking there was no need to reveal that he'd of late been a ramrod there.

The gunman filled a battered mug with coffee. 'How's Crow making out?' he asked, raising the steaming coffee slowly to his lips. 'Is he still around?'

Meaks, for the first time, noticed the slight foreign accent. And then gut instinct told him to keep his mouth shut. He was not going to be the one to tell this man that, yes, Crow was still in Mallory and that Crow would remain permanently in Mallory, planted six foot under.

'There's a fellow named Crow sheep herding,' Meaks croaked, resisting the urge to deny all knowledge of him.

'Sheep herding!' the man guffawed with laughter. 'Damn it, don't that beat all, gentleman Ben sheep herding.'

'Are you fixing to blast Crow?' Meaks heard himself ask, perhaps unwisely, for this sort took umbrage easily.

'Nope,' the other rejoined. 'Although I dare say Crow will want to blast me.'

'You're his pard!'

The other smiled, 'Ben would disagree. Thanks for the coffee and chicken.'

'You're welcome.' Meaks gripped his rifle. 'You're welcome er . . . '

'Linelli,' the other supplied with a feral grin.

Meaks knew the name and he saw the pride the other man took in it. Meaks felt as though he'd been punched in the gut. Bacon was a dead man. And he himself had only been saved because his quest for Miss Dorothy had taken him out of Mallory in the nick of time. Linelli would not trouble himself tracking down a no-account ramrod, but had that ramrod still been around in Mallory no doubt Linelli would have troubled himself.

'Ride out first, pilgrim,' Linelli ordered. 'Not that I don't trust you, but sometimes I get a powerful itch between the shoulder blades.'

Meaks was heartily relieved that he was able to ride out. Without a word he packed up hastily knowing Linelli would attribute the haste to the effect of his name. As Meaks rode out, he found that he itched himself between the shoulder blades, not that Linelli had any reason to want to back shoot him.

Linelli rode on towards Mallory whistling cheerfully. Ben Crow, a stinking sheep herder! That had made his day. There was a range war raging in Wyoming Territory. Maybe Ben would see sense and throw in his lot. Hell, he'd haul Ben out of there by force if he had to, no way could he leave Crow herding sheep. He laughed again, the ugly son of a bitch whose food he'd just eaten forgotten.

* * *

Ben found himself riding back towards San Paulo. Gonzalez' mine would keep for a few days more. A few days would make no difference, unless of course you were a luckless bastard on the wrong side of the wire.

Ben found himself interested to see Gonzalez. Just once. And maybe Escorpión would be around. He had not exactly forgotten about Miss Dorothy, but right now there was little he could do for her. He couldn't save her until he'd killed Escorpión. Meaks, now, he would not forget about Miss Dorothy for one instant. Meaks, of course, was a fool. Even so, Ben would not like to hear that Meaks had been torched by Escorpión.

* * *

Meaks reached the snaking ribbon of muddy water without mishap. Sourly he surveyed the border, for such was this river. They would have come this way, those who had taken Miss Dorothy. Not, of course, to this very spot but the outlaw band would have crossed nearby.

His scowl deepened as he observed that the flow was swifter today. Not that it was a problem; he had crossed faster flowing rivers than this one. Urging his horse into the water; he thought about Bacon. Dead by now, Meaks reckoned, sensing that Linelli would not have cared to linger.

'Hell!' Meaks exclaimed, as too late he saw the danger he was in. Bearing down upon him, its twisted branches outstretched, was a tree. A big one. Meaks tried to urge his horse forward in an attempt to avoid the obstacle, but, of course, it was of little use; the current being far too strong for the animal to make sufficient progress.

'Hell and damnation,' Meaks roared,

as the wood struck his horse. Even as he yelled, he slipped his booted feet free of the stirrups and as his horse went under Meaks managed to separate himself from his saddle.

Water filled his mouth, nostrils and eyes. The waterlogged weight of his clothing and boots sought to pull him down. His arms flailed wildly, his legs kicked but the thought of Miss Dorothy kept him going. If he drowned, her misery continued; she was a gonner, as good as dead, but he was going to save her.

Exhausted, Meaks hauled himself out of the water. He collapsed upon the shale which bordered the river. He lay, face pressed against the shale, arms outstretched, unable to find the strength even to lift his head. His stomach heaved and he spewed out the water he had swallowed.

'I ain't done for,' he grunted, refusing to admit that being on foot with a water-soaked and useless gun was hardly encouraging.

Someone laughed. 'Oh yes, *señor*. You are done for.'

Meaks came up on his knees. The bastards had been there all the time, watching as he'd hauled himself half drowned out of this damn river and neither had troubled to lend a helping hand. Had his .45 been functional he would have shot them both there and then.

Meaks spewed out some more water. They laughed. Meaks let them laugh. Slowly he straightened, his hand reaching down towards his boot. Any fool could see what he was about, but these two were only peons. He drew the knife fast and hurled it with deadly accuracy and had the satisfaction of seeing his blade burying itself in the larger man's throat.

The smaller of the two shot and missed and then Meaks was upon him, hands wrestling for the gun. It was then, just as Meaks knew victory was his, the world went dark as something hard and heavy struck the back of his head.

Back East as Benjamin Crowther, Ben had attended service each Sunday. Since heading West he had not set foot inside a church. It would have been inappropriate somehow. He did not intend to set foot inside church today and yet here he was lounging against a wall opposite the grand cathedral of San Paulo. And he was here because he was curious to see who he was up against.

Escorpión might show up with Gonzalez. Stranger things had happened. And Ben would be able to recognize Gonzalez because the kowtowing De Bois was sure to be in attendance.

Ben stuck a cigar between his lips and waited. Pretty soon the black-robed cleric emerged to welcome his congregation. De Bois was one of the last to arrive.

With De Bois was a fancy-dressed little greaseball who must be Gonzalez and a pretty though fat-looking girl who had to be Gonzalez' daughter and De Bois' intended.

'Well I do declare,' Ben murmured. 'Bet the no-account varmint dyes his hair.' The black hair plastered to Gonzalez' scalp most clearly had been dyed. A paunch bulged above his grey trousers threatening to burst out of the white silk shirt.

Catching the girl's eye Ben winked. He also caught the eye of De Bois. De Bois's neck began to turn brick red with anger as clearly he recalled his last encounter with Ben Crow.

He was so enraged he failed to notice that Elena Gonzalez looked pleased with the fact that a saddle-bum had winked at her.

Crazy Ben Crow here, De Bois thought? Crow must be crazy. He had burnt the monster's old grandma and forced the sister to go crawling to Gonzalez upon her knees. Fear kept De Bois's mouth shut. He could not divulge the man Gonzalez and Amigo wanted so badly was here but a stone's throw away sucking upon a cigar and propping up a wall.

Ben watched as the three disappeared into the dark recess of the cathedral. Gonzalez had not come to town alone; two hardcases had been toted along for protection. Ben knew he ought to move on, but a streak of obstinacy kept him planted.

He found himself almost hoping the two hardcases across the square would try to goad him into reacting. Nothing would give him greater pleasure than blasting the scum associated with Gonzalez, but at the same time his conscience would not allow him to make the first move.

Flies droned; the sun continued to shine, and inside Gonzalez' silver mine men continued to toil in fetid darkness.

'That just ain't right, that just ain't right,' Ben murmured. An old woman hobbling past him leaning heavily on her stick gave him a curious glance. No doubt she saw him as just another crazy bum who'd started talking to himself.

'You might be right, you might be right,' Ben croaked, right about him being crazy.

A small, mangy, brown and white cur ran into the square. It stood still and made the mistake of barking. Ben knew what was coming as one of the hardcases laughingly drew his gun. Ben didn't even think about it. He reached for his own weapon and blasted the gun out of the Mexican's hand, maybe taking part of the hand away with it.

Unfortunately, the second Mexican chose to reach. Ben shot him through the gun arm. Coming to his senses, Ben retreated hurriedly. He darted down a side alleyway. The stink of garbage assailed his nostrils and a rat scuttled across his path. Ben kept going. Well, he had done what he had not intended to do: he had drawn attention to himself, and he guessed pretty soon De Bois would order his soldiers to hunt the murderously inclined gringo bum down.

'This ain't right,' Meaks grunted.

He felt as though the top of his head was coming off. His skull throbbed with pain. Why, Meaks had seen a man struck down in such fashion and afterwards the unlucky galoot couldn't remember his own name.

Meaks knew who he was. He was Pat Meaks and he was in Mexico to save Miss Dorothy. So here he was on his knees, his wrists roped tightly together and a 'hangman's' noose around his neck with a Mex named Carlos gripping the other end of the rope.

Through narrowed eyes, Meaks studied the two. They weren't peons and that was a fact. These two *hombres* fairly bristled with weaponry. Meaks's Spanish was passable and he was disturbed to hear Carlos say that Gonzalez must be told they had the man.

Not a man who had knifed and killed a peon and tried to strangle another, but the man. It was the way Carlos said *the man* which filled Meaks with unease. Carlos made it sound as though they had themselves someone special. A wanted man. One who had maybe crossed Gonzalez, whoever he might be.

'On your feet, gringo,' Carlos commanded arrogantly.

Knowing to argue would be futile and dangerous, Meaks, with a groan of pain, lurched to his feet. For a moment the world spun crazily around him, everything moved; land, rocks, men, horses and even the sky. Somehow or other he managed to stay on his feet.

'You will walk, gringo,' Carlos jeered, as he mounted his horse. 'And if you cannot walk I will drag you until there is nothing but raw meat left.'

'Damn Mex,' Meaks snarled, forgetting his resolve to stay silent. He spat to show his contempt.

For a moment it looked as if Carlos would either shoot him or strike him. A muscle beneath Carlos's eye twitched. And then he laughed, a harsh grating laugh.

'I pray you are the man, *señor*,'

Carlos hissed. 'But even if you are not you will pay for that insult.'

Meaks spat again. After all it looked as if he had nothing to lose. Whatever he did he was damned.

Carlos who had retrieved Meaks's knife from the dead man's throat proceeded to wipe the blade on his pants. Already the dead peon's gaping wound was covered beneath a moving carpet of black and green, the flies having materialized as they always did.

Meaks realized that these two were not going to trouble themselves even to pile rocks on the dead man. The one Meaks had been about to strangle had made himself scarce.

'Fools!' Carlos shrugged. 'When will these peons learn they cannot do a man's work. Now walk, gringo, walk or be dragged until you either choke or become like a piece of raw meat.'

Meaks walked. Pretty soon he stopped wondering where they were taking him. All he could think about was swinging first one foot and then the other. Muscles in his legs which were seldom used — for Meaks, like most cowhands, seldom walked — protested plenty. And his boots must have been shrunk by the river because they pinched his toes like they'd never been pinched before.

He knew Carlos wanted him to fall. He was counting on it. Carlos wanted a chance to rope drag him. Any moment Meaks expected to see him dig in his spurs; the horse would leap forward and that would be the end of Pat Meaks.

Maybe Carlos's pard thought likewise for the two men held a whispered conversation. Meaks heard the name Amigo. And then Carlos, with a harsh laugh actually slowed his pace.

Sweat poured down Meaks's face. His eyes were screwed tight and he practically crawled up the low hill which had blocked their path.

He was only vaguely aware that they had halted.

'Look, gringo. Look,' Carlos ordered,

and there was an unpleasant note in his voice which caused Meaks to force his lids open. Meaks squinted down at the scene below. His view was good. Meaks didn't want to look, but he could not turn his gaze away from the horrific scene.

'Son of a bitch,' Meaks croaked; there being nothing else he could say. 'Son of a bitch,' he reiterated and then threw in, 'Dirty stinking bastard', for good measure.

The son of a bitch to whom Meaks had referred wore, despite the heat, a bright red jacket covered with much gold braid. He rode a white horse, boasted a big sombrero and in his hand he held a burning brand. He held the brand aloft as he circled the stake.

'Son of a bitch,' Meaks said yet again, for tied to that stake, kindling piled around him up to the knees, was a ragged figure.

The place was some sort of a mine Meaks realized, taking in that some of the better-fed and better-dressed *hombres* held rifles and whips. The others were shackled.

With a war whoop, red jacket began to gallop around the stake. Leaning low in the saddle he torched the kindling.

Meaks heard the desperate shriek of fear and pain.

Carlos laughed. 'That, *señor*, is Amigo. Come. I think he would like to meet you.'

# 7

De Bois had more reasons than Gonzalez could imagine for wanting Crow dead. However, he hid his feelings behind an ingratiating smile. 'Too much time has elapsed.' He shrugged apologetically. 'My men did their utmost.'

'The lazy dogs did not stir themselves.' Gonzalez shovelled food into his mouth. 'But no matter, Franco. It is better that our friend Amigo finds this man.' His eyes hardened. 'I do not know this man.'

'Well he knows you, Papa,' Elena chirped up, 'or he knows of you,' she amended. 'Who can he be?' she asked innocently.

Both men ignored her.

'It's been a bad day,' Gonzalez grumbled. 'Those fools summoned me to the mine and for what? So that I could see the wrong man.'

Elena sipped her wine. The news that Carlos had captured the man her father sought had thrown her into panic. She had been greatly relieved when Gonzalez had returned raving that Carlos was a fool. Elena decided she would leave her bedroom window open in the hope that Papa's enemy would appear during the night and carry her away. She'd stay awake for him which meant she must nap this afternoon.

Neither Gonzalez or De Bois thought anything of the vacant expression upon Elena's plump face, although it did occur to Gonzalez his daughter must be unwell for she hardly ate anything of her meal.

Oblivious to the fact that he was featuring predominantly in Elena Gonzalez' thoughts, Ben waited until darkness fell and the night wore on.

The pursuit had been desultory, the young conscripts having no wish to run themselves into the ground. Seasoned troops and a good tracker might have been able to run him to earth but not these greenhorns. He was glad of it. He would not have wanted to shoot any of them.

Riding from San Paulo, he'd decided to go ahead with his foolhardy plan. He'd been unable to think of any other way to hit Gonzalez hard where it hurt. And if he hit Gonzalez he'd hit Escorpión. The two men were linked by more than money.

Gonzalez' weakness was his hirelings at the mine. They were paid to keep men behind wire and that was precisely what they did. That anyone would want to come through the wire into the mine had not occurred to any of them. At night the varmints fell down on the job and Ben aimed to exploit this failing.

Tonight he would pay the Elena Gonzalez silver mine a second call and this time they'd know he'd been around.

His horse tethered some distance

from the mine, Ben got down on his belly and with some difficulty began to snake his way towards the mine. He feared to rise lest he present a target in the darkness. It was a long shot, but maybe Gonzalez was expecting a night attack and maybe he'd set a trap.

The desert night was cool and quiet save for the slight rustling sounds which always came with the night. Then the stillness was broken by the soft and throaty laughter of a woman. A shrill giggle and a squeal followed the laughter. Ben smiled in the darkness. There were lights showing from the guard-house and he guessed he knew what Gonzalez' guards were getting up to. None of them would be venturing out to patrol the wire fence when entertainment was clearly being provided within.

He guessed a wagonful of sporting women had been shipped in to while away the boredom that went with this kind of work.

'Damnit,' he muttered. That was

what he ought to be doing himself. Enjoying himself. And here he was crawling along in the dark too cautious to walk like a man. But hell, it was better to crawl than to burn and that would be his fate if he fell into the hands of Gonzalez and Escorpión.

He tried to fill his head with thoughts about the last woman he'd been with because inexplicably he'd found himself thinking of scorpions. He found himself worrying in case he ran into one of the little varmints.

Ben had once seen the result of a scorpion's sting. He knew just how the swelling bloated the skin until it looked near bursting point and then the bloated skin would turn black. Ben swallowed. He'd overlooked vicious red-legged centipedes and blister bugs and . . .

A rattle broke the stillness. And rattlesnakes, Ben concluded fighting his incipient panic. Hell, these perils were rattling him more than the thought of Escorpión. He strained his ears. The rattle hadn't sounded particularly close at hand. Instinctively he clenched his hand and pulled it close to his body. He told himself that rattlers didn't go hunting people, but the thought didn't help.

'What the hell.' He forced a grin and forced himself to move forward once more. He'd been near enough dead and had been spared. Of course, fate could have dealt him a bum hand, but he was prepared to bet that he would die with his boots off.

His grin became a parody. 'Yeah, here and now, bitten on the hand or face by some goddamn rattlesnake.'

* * *

Meaks lay in the fetid darkness oblivious to the snorts, grunts and moans of his fellow captives. He was going mad with thirst. When the other prisoners had been watered that bastard Carlos had kicked the small tin bowl out of Meaks's manacled hands.

133

'I want to see you mad with thirst,' Carlos had hissed. 'I want to see you throw yourself upon the wire. You know the penalty for attempting to escape? Amigo will burn you. No one has ever escaped from this place.'

'That's nice to know,' Meaks had managed to rejoin although his guts felt as though they were in his boots.

Meaks was unable to forget the paralysing fear which had washed over him when this red-coated Amigo had fixed him with two round, cold, snake eyes.

'He is not the one,' Amigo had said, and then with a shrug had turned away.

'But he's a gringo,' Carlos had protested.

'My friend.' Amigo had regarded Carlos mockingly. 'Do you see a handsome blond-headed *hombre* with a damaged throat? A *hombre* who'd been hung until the rope bit into his throat? No, you see a bald-headed, ugly son of a bitch and still you persist. Your brains are addled, Carlos. You are a fool. Say it.'

'I am a fool,' Carlos had muttered, his eyes filled with shame and hatred.

'Louder,' Amigo had ordered.

Whilst that little pantomime had been taking place Meaks had lowered his head lest anyone observe his shock. The description fitted Ben Crow. It could be no other. Which meant the lawman, Strike, had lied. Crow was not lying six foot under but here somewhere in Mexico raising a hornets' nest.

Meaks found the presence of mind to clamp his jaws which had dropped open in surprise tightly shut. He knew why Crow was in Mexico, he was after Miss Dorothy. He intended hauling her back and making her admit she'd lied. Or maybe Crow just aimed to blast her. But where Crow was concerned Meaks knew he could not make assumptions.

But why the hell, he wondered, had Crow locked horns with this here Gonzalez? Surely a rich mine owner would not be behind a stage robbery? And then it had struck him like a blow that maybe this monster Amigo was the one who'd taken Miss Dorothy. Quite clearly, Amigo was Gonzalez' hireling.

'Put the dog to work,' Amigo ordered.

A rawhide whip struck Meaks across the back. 'You heard Amigo,' someone taunted.

Now, as Meaks lay in the darkness, his shirt shredded and bloodied for he had been struck more than once, he relived his nightmare.

He'd been herded into a wooden cage. The windlass had creaked as they had descended into Hell; so much so Meaks had thought they would plunge to their death. But it was not to be. And the more the cage descended the hotter it became.

As Meaks had stumbled out of the cage, he'd been handed a candle lantern and a pickaxe. Filth of all description covered the floor and the rock was hot beneath his feet. He found himself hardly able to breathe and he had a hunch that a man's lungs wouldn't last overlong in this hell. Not that anyone up top would give a damn. Men would be worked until they dropped and then replaced.

As Meaks swung his pickaxe, he was forced to admit that his only hope of getting out was Ben Crow. Ben Crow, the man he'd help lynch maybe might save his hide. Not that Ben Crow could be expected knowingly to lift a hand to save Pat Meaks, but unknowingly perhaps.

Meaks filled his handcart. Immediately it was pushed away by a scrawny wretch too feeble to wield a pickaxe. A fresh handcart was pushed into place and the cut of the whip set Meaks's pickaxe swinging again.

★ ★ ★

Reaching the outer barbed-wire fence, Ben carefully cut his way through. All true cowhands hated barbed wire so beloved by dirtbusters. No cowhand, Ben understood why the wire was loathed. Cursing softly, for a strand caught his jacket, Ben wriggled beneath the wire.

Oddly he was relaxed. Seemingly, scorpions, centipedes and rattlers were not out to get him, leastways, he had not encountered any. He'd made it through safely, reaching the second fence. Ben got to work.

The laughter was louder now. Men hooted and cheered and shouted profanities whilst others stamped their feet. They were having one hell of a time which made his raid, for raid it was, easier.

But he was over confident. A light flared in the darkness directly before him for he had crawled through facing the guard house. Hell, he thought, someone preferred a cigar to women. And never had it taken a galoot so long to smoke a cigar. Ben's nose twitched. He feared he was going to sneeze. By the time the guard had ground the stub into the dust, Ben had begun to sweat.

Light spilled out through the wide-open guard-house door affording Ben a tantalizing glimpse of a woman naked except for black stockings. Ben guessed that before they'd be able to come rushing out they'd need to find discarded clothing and boots, not to mention weapons. Drunk as skunks, he doubted any of them would be able to shoot straight.

He crawled on, reached the third wire fence, cut the wire and then he was inside Gonzalez' mine. It had been his intention to blow the guardhouse sky high, but with women inside he guessed he'd have to forego that particular pleasure.

He'd settled for the mine itself.

Bending low, Ben raced for the gaping mouth of the Elena Gonzalez Mine. He'd bring the roof down. That would halt production for a while and it would sure as hell rouse Gonzalez.

That bastard Escorpión would be

mounting a man hunt pretty damn quick which suited Ben just fine. He'd deal with Escorpión and then save Miss Dorothy. But what the hell was he going to do with her once he'd saved her?

This thought left him with a powerful headache.

He reached the entrance to the mine without being challenged. Squatting, he opened his gunny sack and searched around for candles. He even started to whistle softly and cheerfully. He was here, still in one piece. He hadn't blown himself sky high. Of course, he still might do that, but he didn't give a damn for he knew what dying was all about. Not many could say that.

He lit his candles, careful where he placed them. And then got out his dynamite. The yellow flames cast shadows on the wall. Ben did not doubt that he would get clear in time for he was laying very long, slow-burning fuses.

If the mine did not blow he would

not be fool enough to go back and investigate. That would be stretching his luck a mite too far. He lit the fuses and ran, this time not troubling about whether there was anyone around to spot him.

In his haste to roll beneath the first wire fence a barbed strand tore his forehead. He felt his warm blood trickling down his face; but he did not let the feeling slow him down. Moving and rolling, he cleared the second fence.

As he raced for the third a shot rang out. Ben had a hunch it was the cigar smoker out for another puff. Clearing the third fence, Ben cast a glance over his shoulder. He spotted a dark shape running not towards the wire fencing but towards the shed where the prisoners were housed. The fool believed one of the prisoners had gotten out so it therefore followed if one was out maybe more were on the loose.

Ben raced towards a shrub. Behind, in the darkness, he heard muffled curses and then another shot was fired, way off target, probably to rouse the rest of the drunken bums.

* * *

In the prison shed, Meaks strained his ears. He heard the shouts and counted two shots. It sounded to Meaks as though the guard were shouting a prisoner was escaping which was nonsense.

The explosion came before Meaks had time to think further. The noise made Meaks think of the end of the world. Rocks rained down striking the prison shed whilst the miserable inhabitants cowered on the floor in the choking blackness covering their heads with scrawny arms.

'Goddamnit!' Meaks exclaimed. It had to be Crow. This was his work. The crazy bastard had blown up the Elena Gonzalez Mine.

Elena Gonzalez herself heard what she took to be the distant roll of thunder.

The sound displeased her exceedingly. Quite rightly, Elena reasoned her man of mystery would not come climbing through her open window to carry her away should there be a torrential downpour outside. However, much to her relief, the rain did not materialize.

But what did occur some time later was the sounds of men and horses outside the ranch house. Loud voices yelled for her papa. She pricked up her ears for the voices were yelling that the mine had been blown up. The roof was down and the workings were inoperable.

Whilst her father screeched in fury, Elena worked out the implications of what she had heard. She was quite put out when she realized Papa's enemy would not be coming for her. He'd gone to the mine. And after tonight Papa would have guards patrolling the ranch house which would make it quite impossible for her to be carried off.

★ ★ ★

Meaks reached up and managed to grip the bars fronting the narrow slit which served as a window. Even prisoners needed air and these slit windows ran the length of the wall facing towards the guardhouse and the mine. Gripping the bars tightly, Meaks, whose muscular shoulders had not yet lost their power, was able to raise himself by bending his arms and was thus able to look out.

At first he had witnessed the departure of the frightened, crying women, dishevelled, hair unpinned, war paint smeared. They'd been booted out of the camp — literally, for the guards had kicked those of them slow to board the wagon taking them back to town.

It was quite clear the bastards were running scared. And given what went on inside this hell-hole Meaks guessed the guards had every reason to fear the wrath of their employer, for they had failed spectacularly to safeguard Gonzalez' investment.

Edward Bacon had been a ruthless son of a bitch but he was as nothing when compared to these two. Meaks thought of Bacon in the past for he was pretty sure Crow's erstwhile 'pard' would have dealt with Bacon by now.

Peering out, Meaks had a limited vision of the guards standing stiffly to attention, clutching rifles and whips as though their lives depended on the strength of their grips. If the prison shed had not stunk like a cesspit Meaks reckoned he would have been able to smell the stink of fear the guards were giving off, for Gonzalez and Amigo were both here.

Meaks ignored the strain in his shoulders as he sought to see what happened next. The little greaseball Gonzalez he saw had turned up wearing a purple satin waistcoat. And now he began to strut back and forth like a puffed-up chicken whilst he surveyed the damage done to his mine. Amigo, still wearing his fancy red coat, showed little interest in the damage, seemingly content to smoke his cigar.

In his far from perfect Spanish,

Meaks related what he could see. Unwashed bodies pressed closely around him for the unlucky men were desperate to know what was happening outside.

I'd bet my boots there'll be another burning, Meaks thought. Hell, that puffed-up, no-account little bum is sure to find himself a scapegoat. Meaks felt a surge of hope when Gonzalez stopped before Carlos.

Carlos looked uneasy now whilst his pards appeared clearly relieved. It followed, Meaks reasoned, that Gonzalez could not dispose of all his guards no matter how inclined he must be feeling so to do. Carlos, it seemed, had drawn the short straw.

And that meant that Pat Meaks had a chance to live a mite longer. Denied his water supply by the vicious, vindictive Carlos, Meaks had known that he'd be dead before too long had passed.

Amigo was filled with a sense of exhilaration. He could not help but feel a sneaking admiration for the unknown man. Gonzalez' enemy — and a ruthless enemy to boot. A man after his own heart, for this man had not hesitated to strike at the heart of Gonzalez, his profitable mine. But Amigo would find and burn him notwithstanding the admiration.

With amused contempt, Amigo watched Carlos squirm. He wondered why the fool did not at least try to kill Gonzalez whilst there was still opportunity. Amigo frowned. He hoped the hunt for the unknown enemy would be over quickly for he was anxious to get back to Miss Dorothy. Even now she would be plotting against him, thinking of how she might kill him.

Gonzalez, the centre of attention, continued to berate Carlos loudly with particular emphasis upon how Carlos had betrayed his trust. And then coming to an abrupt halt, Gonzalez snapped two podgy fingers.

It was the signal the two men he had primed had been waiting for. Standing on either side of Carlos, they lunged at him and brought him down before he had a chance to realize what was intended. As they were men he knew and trusted, as much as he was able to trust anyone, he was taken completely by surprise and did not have the chance to reach for his pistol.

'No. Not the stake, I beg you,' Carlos howled, sending a shiver down Meaks's spine.

Gonzalez laughed. 'Not the stake; Carlos. No. I have something else in mind for you.'

A surprised Meaks watched as Carlos, minus his weapons, was frog-marched towards the prison shed.

'Goddamnit!' Meaks exclaimed. 'I reckon they're bringing him here.'

Meaks dropped to the floor aware that an expectant hush had fallen within the prison shed. It occurred to Meaks the poor bastards might have the idea to rush the open door but then he dismissed the notion. No one would be doing any rushing. Everyone was shackled at the feet. All they could do was shuffle.

The door opened. A flare of light streamed into the gloom and then Carlos was thrust roughly into the shed. A bolt slammed shut behind him.

Hoarse, animal yells broke out as the miserable wretches moved in on Carlos. For a while he succeeded in avoiding contact, but then he was grabbed and brought down. Unwashed bodies surged forward and covered him.

Meaks sagged back against the wall. He did not need to see what was going on. They were tearing Carlos to pieces.

# 8

It was a big risk returning to San Paulo, but it was a risk Ben was prepared to take.

He needed to send a telegram.

Just thinking about the content of his telegram made him laugh.

He entered San Paulo without being challenged. Just another down-at-heel bum. He even rode past two slouching soldiers without being challenged. Clearly De Bois had not troubled to circulate his description. To do so would be to admit to a knowledge De Bois was keen to deny.

Ben dismounted outside the telegraph office. Patiently he waited his turn behind two fat old women smelling strongly of garlic. The clerk even went so far as to shrug apologetically as the two dithered, but finally they were gone.

'Send this.' Ben placed his paper on

the cigarmarked counter.

'*Si señor.*' The clerk evinced little interest in Ben or his message. In fact, he went so far as to light himself a cheroot before glancing at Ben's message. Then the cigar fell from the man's thick lips and lay unheeded, burning upon the counter.

'But, *señor*, I cannot send this!' he exclaimed, aghast.

'Sure you can,' Ben rasped.

'No, *señor*, no.'

'Because if you refuse I'll just have to kill you,' Ben concluded, face hard.

Evidently his expression was mean enough to convince the clerk for the man nodded vigorously. With a hand not quite steady, the clerk rapidly tapped out the message.

'Feel free to inform De Bois.'

The clerk shook his head more vigorously than before. 'That, *señor*, I will not do. I will be held accountable for this. If not by De Bois then by others.' He retrieved his cigar and took a long pull.

'Ever heard of the three wise monkeys? See no evil, speak no evil, hear no evil.' Ben grinned. 'Well; the folk of San Paulo kind of remind me of those monkeys. I reckon you all know what this Gonzalez and Amigo are about.'

'If you know, *señor*, you would be wise to ride and ride far,' the clerk advised. He shrugged. 'But, no, I think you will stay.'

Ben nodded. He turned away and went out into the street. He ought to get out of town now that he had achieved his objective, but hell, he wasn't going without a drink. Having that drink would prove that he wasn't running scared. He stood for a moment in the sunshine and then turned down one of the narrow cobbled alleyways. He felt safer away from the main square of the town. The cantinas would be cool and dark and perhaps the overheard talk would be interesting.

He ducked into a dark inviting doorway and found himself a corner table. Leaning back, he tilted his worn boots on the table, in common with other customers he noted, and raised his drink to his lips. The fiery liquid burned his throat. And the burning made him remember that polecat Edward Bacon and his fool of a ramrod, Meaks. Why, if Meaks had voiced his passion, Ben was sure Miss Dorothy would have had him up before a preacher pretty damn quick.

Two oldsters tottered in from the alleyway. Leaning heavily on sticks painfully they made their way to the table nearest to Ben. It soon became clear to Ben that the two old coots knew all about the Elena Gonzalez Mine and its slave workforce, for one of the old fools obstinately maintained that Gonzalez' miners did not know the meaning of true work and toil. They were having an easy time of it.

Ben hurriedly took a gulp of his drink. It stopped him trying to shake sense into the two idiots. Clearly these two had been nowhere near the mine. No one was fool enough to trespass on

Gonzalez land. It took a while before Ben realized that these two had once worked another mine, a place back in the hills which had yielded a good return way back.

'Where the hell is this place?' Ben interrupted the disjointed sentences. He'd had another crazy idea. His first crazy idea had been to blow up the Gonzalez mine, the second idea was just as crazy and might work.

Two wrinkled faces turned towards him. They reminded him of two old tortoises, but in reality they'd be snakes: Gonzalez would hear of his interest. It would pay Gonzalez to have eyes and ears in town, men who would betray for the sight of a coin.

Lips parted in toothless smiles. 'Do you want something, *señor*?' the oldster asked.

Ben produced a bill. 'I'd be grateful for information,' he rejoined.

'You have a sore throat, *señor*,' the old man cackled. 'So you have almost seen the Devil.'

'We missed one another,' Ben rejoined, 'but there's a devil hereabouts so I've heard.'

Both wrinkled faces grew wary. No one volunteered any information about Amigo.

'The Devil is everywhere, *señor*. He tempts us and leads us . . . '

'Just tell me the whereabouts of this mine.' Ben didn't want to discuss the Devil. He winked. 'You old coots will be meeting him soon I reckon.'

The remark was not well received. 'Perhaps you will meet him soon, *señor*. Perhaps you will meet both devils.' When Ben failed to respond, the oldster rattled off directions which would take Ben to the unnamed long abandoned mine.

'Can you remember, *señor*?' The old man pocketed the note with alacrity.

Ben nodded. 'I sure can old-timer. You tell the Devil and his pard I'll be seeing them around.' He was glad he'd come into the cantina. Things are coming together, so Linelli often declared. And Ben guessed that they were.

'You!' the harsh voice halted his progress.

Two hardcases stood by the door about to enter as he'd been on his way to exit. Fate sure as hell had played another trick. A minute or two sooner he would have missed them. Now a hunch told him that he would have to kill them, because if he did not he would not be able to leave San Paulo alive.

They had dead eyes, he thought, noticing how they wore their guns tied low. One of them, the man who had challenged him, wore vicious silver star spurs on the side of red boots.

'You!' Silver Spur accused. 'You are the man Gonzalez seeks.'

And you, Ben thought, are the man I am going to kill. Nevertheless, he tried to avoid the inevitable. 'I have no fight with you,' he rasped. He wondered how fast on the draw these two were. Any moment now he would find out.

'Gonzalez wants your head.' Silver Spur wanted to prolong the moment. He had everyone's attention. Ben knew his kind: attention seekers always played with their victims first. 'You stink. I can smell your fear.'

Ben's right hand trembled slightly as if to confirm his fear. He used this trick before. It always worked.

Silver Spur's companion, lips pulled back to reveal yellowing teeth, spat. His gob of tobacco landed on the scuffed toe of Ben's boot. It was the last thing he ever did, for already Ben's left hand was moving towards the butt of his pistol. Ben never bothered with the nonsense of letting the opponent make the first move, he wasn't that good. His first bullet hit the spitter through the forehead and his second struck Silver Spur in the belly, just above the big fancy buckle of his belt.

It was over. Ben stood, smoking .45 in his hand, eyes watchful as he waited for someone to move. No one did.

'Tolerable shooting, stranger,' the

oldster he'd been speaking with but a moment before cackled. 'But if those fools had not wanted to talk you'd be dead meat. Talk is for the old.'

'Well, they cannot do much else,' a bold-eyed, black-haired girl quipped. She stepped towards Ben who was backing warily towards the door, 'Now, don't you be fool enough to stop off at the bath house on your way out of town,' she admonished. 'Save it for when you come back. I'll be waiting. It's on the house.'

'You damn fool.' Ben shoved her to one side. 'Don't you know better than to get between a man and those who might want to blast him?'

Her face told him she hadn't thought of that possibility.

She looked appealing in her low-cut, bright orange dress Ben thought, the idea coming to him that when this was over he might just come back to this cantina. He nodded slightly and she flashed him a smile.

'Just ask for Concita.'

The dying man on the floor howled with pain. No one paid him any attention.

'Five dollars he does not come back for Concita,' someone cried.

'Ten that he does,' another responded.

Ben exited into the street. As he rode out of San Paulo he saw that the telegraph office had been locked and closed. On account of illness, the sign said. It figured; the clerk had decided to make himself scarce. It was a wise decision.

Using the back alleyways to get clear of the town, Ben rode out of San Paulo. Soon Gonzalez would know where he was bound. Then he would send Amigo and it would be over one way or another.

He frowned. Miss Dorothy might not be pleased to see him of all folk. That crazy female might even try to knife him herself. Had being Amigo's prisoner driven her mad? Of course, some might argue that she was mad already, mad and passing herself off

159

as sane all these years. He'd save the woman and then put her on the nearest train or stage and he'd feel a whole lot happier being rid of her.

He brought his thoughts back to the present. Even now someone from the cantina would be riding to inform Gonzalez of what had occurred.

* * *

Gonzalez looked down at the two dead men. Both were naked. He knew that jackal of an undertaker had removed their clothes. His sister washed and patched them and then they were sold.

Gonzalez rubbed his chin. The corpses were unpleasant to view. Especially the one who'd had his head blown off. It had been no mean feat killing these two. Once again the blond American killer had proved his mettle.

It irked Gonzalez not knowing who his enemy might be. It enraged him that the two dead men could have killed the American but had messed up. In his opinion they deserved to be dead.

Gonzalez had never wanted a man dead as much as he wanted this unknown gringo dead. It had occurred to him that the man had been hired to destroy him. He had many enemies.

The question uppermost in his mind was what the hell was this crazy man going to do next. If Gonzalez only knew the answer to that he would have his enemy at his mercy.

Leaving the undertakers, with three thuggish bodyguards dogging his heels, he made his way to the cantina. It was here that he hoped to learn the answer to his question. The *patron* had sent him word, not because he was loyal to Gonzalez but because he knew that Gonzalez would have had the place burnt down with himself inside if the information had not been sent.

The old men with whom the gringo had spoken still sat at their table now making a pretence of playing dominoes.

Wrinkled faces turned towards him. Contemptuously, Gonzalez dropped a coin upon the table.

'Well!' he demanded.

A gnarled hand closed over the coin. 'There is not much to tell, *patron*,' the old man replied. 'The stranger merely asked about the mine I once worked at as a boy. He wanted directions. Directions I gave him. That is all.'

'And his name?' Gonzalez essayed.

For a moment the old man looked at Gonzalez as if he were a fool. 'He did not give a name, *patron*. Nor did I ask. It is not wise.' The old man laughed. 'Perhaps this gringo feels a need to blow up mines.'

'Have a care, old man,' Gonzalez threatened. 'I am not amused.'

'My apologies, *patron*.' The old man appeared contrite. Gonzalez turned away in disgust. The old devil found this all amusing.

Gonzalez stood in the alleyway behind the cantina. He shook with anger. But he must, he told himself,

162

try to think as this gringo would think. Surely the gringo would know the old men would not keep silent? Was this talk of the old man a wild goose chase, a trick to deploy men fruitlessly, to waste time, or was this madman intending to use the mine as his lair? He must talk with Amigo.

'I know only one thing.' Amigo had listened in silence. 'Clearly this man wants you dead. If we take men up into the hills, if we seek out this deserted mine, we will leave my camp and your land unguarded.' He gave a sardonic grin. 'Not to mention Elena Gonzalez — I speak of the mine and not your stout daughter. No man would be so foolish as to want to run off with such a one.' He paused. 'I think this man wants you to seek him at the mine. And while you seek he plans to strike again.'

'But I believe he has indeed gone to this mine,' Gonzalez replied. 'And why? Because he believes this mine is the last place we will search. He told everyone he was going so it must follow he did not go.' Gonzalez smiled unpleasantly. 'This man has a devious mind. Continue your search, Amigo. Maintain your vigil, but you will not see him. I will lead my men into the hills. Honour demands it. Had he not blown up the Elena Gonzalez I could have left the task to you.' He shrugged. 'The man will be a long time dying. I plan to skin him, strip by strip.'

'Find out why he wants you dead,' Amigo advised. And then he shrugged. 'But, of course, you cannot find out for you will not find this man. Your search will have the peons sniggering, the more so if you lose your way in the hills. You have become an armchair rancher, Brother. A great disappointment to our late father.'

The two half-brothers glared at each other.

'The fire that killed him was no accident,' Gonzalez snarled.

'It suited you.' Amigo shrugged. 'The ranch was yours.' His eyes narrowed,

'You were too afraid to kill him,' he hissed. 'He treated us both like dogs, but it was I, the bastard, who had the courage to make an end to him.'

'You pray I kill this gringo,' Gonzalez retorted, determined upon the last word.

'Why should I pray?' Amigo was genuinely astonished.

'Because the man is crazy enough to come after you next,' Gonzalez replied.

Amigo smiled. 'Men have always run from me before. Perhaps I would welcome this gringo. I will speak with him before I kill him. I will burn out his eyes and leave him in pain and darkness for a very long time. And then when he is broken I will kill him. But the idea that he will come looking for me is ridiculous.'

Just in time, Elena, who had been eavesdropping at the keyhole, slipped into the library. Stout daughter indeed! And now she'd be worrying about Amigo catching the gringo.

'*Patron, patron*.' The peon knocked hard at the door. 'I have news *patron*, bad news indeed.'

Gonzalez jerked the door open. The hireling almost fell into the room.

'What news?'

'My sister. She cleans at the fort.'

'Well!'

'My sister can read, the good sisters . . . '

Her father deserved to be struck down for what he said about the good sisters, Elena who was back in position, thought.

The peon drew a crumpled sheet of paper from his pocket. 'One of the soldiers is manning the telegraph office, for the clerk is gone. This came for the captain.'

Gonzalez and Amigo read simultaneously.

'He has betrayed us,' Amigo cried in anger. 'De Bois has betrayed us.'

'The captain has wired that the telegram was sent unnecessarily. He does not now need assistance.' The peon gulped. 'But they have left. They have already left, *patron*.'

'You have done well. Take this.' Gonzalez handed the man several bills.

'Thank you, *patron*,' the peon bowed.

Elena slipped back into the library. What fools men were. It occurred to neither of them she might be curious.

'De Bois did not send the telegram,' Gonzalez stated with certainty. 'It was the gringo. That is why the clerk has disappeared. This means, of course, Amigo, that De Bois must make a show of moving against you. You must slip away.'

'You are accused of harbouring a crazed bandit,' Amigo hissed. 'But you will not slip away, will you, Brother? De Bois will find there is insufficient evidence.'

'I'll order him to wait until this business with the gringo has been resolved.'

'Do that.'

Elena remained in the library. Listening. She heard a door open and close, and the sound of footsteps. Her father's. Of considerable bulk, his tread was heavier.

And then there was much commotion with the peons running around like headless chickens. Horses were brought out and saddles. Supplies packed. From the library she had an excellent view. And finally her father himself in his best riding clothes, his boots shining, strode out. He heaved himself into the saddle with an effort she noted.

She had more sense than he. Those inclined to be large tired far more easily. Her own feet ached when she took the dance floor. One had to do less and yet her father was planning a long expedition beneath a burning sun. The air was so oppressive it sucked the energy from the body. Elena cheered considerably; he might suffer a heart attack and die. She wouldn't have to marry De Bois and the ranch would be hers.

She waited in the silence of the library. Then, gathering her courage, returned to the door of her father's study. She placed an eye to the keyhole.

Amigo had gone quite mad. Blade in hand, he was attacking the leather furniture, long, downward, forceful strokes ripped the leather of her father's favourite chair.

She knew with certainty that if her father did come back Amigo would kill him.

# 9

Gonzalez had only ridden a few miles before he began to regret that he had not sent Amigo. Even as a younger man he had not cared to travel on horse-back. Now, older and heavier, the heat and the dust were worse than ever. His discomfort increased as time passed. His thighs were sore and as for his posterior . . . only the thought of having his enemy helpless and at his mercy kept him going. But the extensive area of desert, a region of thorny and leafless vegetation, a sea of dried grass which lay between the company and the mountains looked endless.

He was glad that he had Manolito along with him. Manolito was his head *vaquero* and of all the men, Manolito possessed a streak of cruelty which was akin to Gonzalez' own.

This vicious streak made Manolito particularly effective when it came to breaking the horses needed for ranch work. Manolito liked to girth the unfortunate animals so tightly that their eyes practically bulged from their sockets. Then, armed with a pair of cruel spurs the size of a soup plate and a mesquite club, Manolito would get to work.

Gonzalez decided he would allow Manolito to get to work on the gringo. It would be far more satisfying perhaps to watch the torture being inflicted than to exert himself. There would be much blood and his clothes would become bespattered. Far better to sip his whiskey and smoke his cigar whilst Manolito did the work.

A basking scorpion, black and deadly, caught his eye. Meanness caused Gonzalez to reach for his gun. Taking careful aim he blasted the head. Behind him, Manolito's expression became a sneer; Manolito knew Gonzalez believed that dealing with the gringo would be almost as easy as killing the unsuspecting animal.

Manolito thought differently. Manolito believed the gringo was setting a trap for them. The man had practically invited them to follow him to the mine. He knew they would come and he would be waiting to greet them in his own fashion. He had told Gonzalez this but the *patron* had insisted that the gringo would believe they would not be going to the mine.

Manolito felt uneasy. He knew of this place. His grandfather had laboured there as a young man. It had been a place of sickness and death. Manolito's grandfather had always maintained that the spirits of those who had died inside the mine remained still trapped for ever.

Tonight Manolito would drink his fermented mescal and try not to think of the mine and the gringo. He had a bad feeling about this man. He glared at Gonzalez' broad back; because of the *patron* they travelled slowly. The gringo would have plenty of time in which to set his trap.

Ben's main worry was the possibility that no one would turn up to hunt him down and that he'd be left waiting at the mine whilst time passed with intolerable slowness. Common sense told him that he was worrying unnecessarily, Escorpión would come.

His first act had been to quickly explore the tumble-down cabins once used by the old-time miners. In one of them he'd found to his astonishment battered back and breast plates of silver. And there had been an odd-looking helmet. After a while it had occurred to him that the armour must have belonged to one of the Spanish explorers, although what the foot soldier was doing up in the hills was a mystery. Or maybe the armour was here because one of the miners had simply toted it around from place to place.

Ben also discovered a good many skeletons both in the cabins and inside the mine itself. Tools and utensils had been left behind. The discovery that this place had clearly been stricken by a quick spreading and deadly infectious disease gave him something else to worry about.

Apart from the main entrance with its shaft dropping steeply down, Ben discovered three smaller almost concealed entrances with narrow sloping tunnels down which a man must crawl before he could reach the workings. He guessed the miners themselves had made these tunnels in case there was a cave-in at the main entrance. The place was a rabbit warren with tunnels branching in all directions, but he proceeded slowly and carefully, familiarizing himself with the place, his lantern casting grotesque shadows upon the walls, shadows that bore no resemblance to himself.

However, he was not a fanciful sort nor did he believe he was intended to die here. An amusing thought came to him then as the roof and walls of the tunnel seemed to converge upon him,

174

he thought that if he were to die he'd probably end up with his gizzard slit by an ungrateful Miss Dorothy. The idea made him laugh and banished his fear of the mine.

Gonzalez had tumbled from his horse aching, hot and ill-tempered. But instead of falling into an exhausted slumber he had found himself hardly able to sleep at all. The ground was hard and the howling of the coyotes awoke an urge to exterminate every last one of the four-legged vermin. Around him, his men grunted and snored as he lay awake in the darkness cursing the gringo.

And it seemed that he had hardly fallen asleep before one of his men was shaking him and urging him to rise, for breakfast awaited.

He lurched to his feet. The smell of the coffee was welcome, but the sight of the coarse porridge that he was expected to eat was less than welcoming.

To his left there was a terrible

scream. One of his men, clutching his bare foot rolled on the ground screaming and babbling with terror as he yelled that a scorpion had bitten him.

Gonzalez could not explain why he did it but without thought he drew his gun and shot his own *vaquero*. Twice. Abruptly the howling ceased. There was a sudden shocked and ominous silence.

Manolito sized up the situation. He reacted quickly, yelling out that it was an act of mercy and that the fool was as good as dead anyway. Far better a quick death than to die slowly with a foot swollen and black.

'*Compadres*, we could not have taken him with us. The *patron* had no choice,' Manolito concluded, waving his hands eloquently.

'I had no choice,' Gonzalez reiterated, vaguely alarmed now, aware that he had erred but not aware how much the mistake might cost him. As from this moment whatever loyalty his men might have given him vanished.

Manolito knew that he had only to give a signal and the men would fall upon Gonzalez and literally tear him to pieces. He would have liked to have seen it. But, alas, there were wages to consider and, more importantly, the *patron*'s younger brother Bernardo, the crazy man-burner who went around calling himself Amigo. Amigo might, although not objecting to having his brother killed, might just feel obliged to seek vengeance and they all were aware of the form Amigo's vengeance took.

'Breakfast for the *patron*,' Manolito yelled. The moment of danger passed. A man handed the *patron* a mug of coffee. Gonzalez took his coffee oblivious to how close to death he had been.

★ ★ ★

De Bois patrolled his fort. He always thought of the place as his fort. Troubled, he felt an overwhelming need to walk.

He strode past the officers' quarters, the adjutant's office and the post bakery. He paused for a moment outside the guardhouse and then continued on to the quartermaster's storehouse. The men's quarters and the sutler's store came next. However, he halted outside the butcher's corral. Resting his arms on the wooden rail he stared at the doomed milling cattle.

He was trapped just as they were trapped. Doomed. He had been ordered to march against Amigo. Just as soon as the 'help' arrived. And Hernandez, himself would be leading the extra troops. Hernandez, who had already heard rumours of this bandit with a liking for burning men; Hernandez, who had jumped at the chance to hunt down the bandit and take his head.

De Bois swore. He knew who had sent that damn request for help. Crow, that was who. And he had also figured out why Crow was here. It was not Gonzalez Crow was after, but Amigo.

De Bois knew that when Amigo had

returned from his raid across the border he had brought back a woman. Not a young and pretty woman as might be expected, but a woman who was old and as thin as a stick, a woman who'd killed one of his men and was now trying to kill Amigo himself.

Quite likely if Amigo released Miss Dorothy, Crow would take the woman and go. Although why Crow would want Miss Dorothy was a mystery to De Bois. But, of course, Amigo would not release her, nor would releasing Miss Dorothy solve the problem of Hernandez who would arrive with his own Indian trackers. There was no chance of being able to lead Hernandez round in circles.

De Bois decided to get drunk.

★ ★ ★

From the canyon's rim, Ben, lying flat upon his stomach, watched the canyon floor.

They were coming.

Finally.

And only now did he understand why it was they had been so long in coming. He cursed softly. Winding his way through the canyon was not Amigo at the head of his outlaw band, but Gonzalez leading his *vaqueros*.

It could be argued that Gonzalez' *vaqueros* were surely as bad as their boss. They knew of the slaves mining silver for Gonzalez. Doubtless these men had taken doomed wretches to the mine. They knew of and might have even witnessed the burnings. These men would have voiced no protests at what was going on, but even so Ben was not eager to kill these particular hirelings.

He sighted his rifle meaning now merely to bring Gonzalez down. With him dead he doubted that the *vaqueros* would continue the pursuit. But, as ill luck would have it, Gonzalez' horse, already sagging beneath the bulk it carried, chose that moment to stumble. The animal went down, flanks heaving, bit flecked with foam, pushed to the limit of its endurance by the monster it carried.

And amazingly Gonzalez managed to clear the stirrups and fall away from the horse even as Ben squeezed the trigger. More amazingly, Gonzalez possessed the savvy to stay put. He used the bulk of his dying horse as a shield.

The chance to end things now was lost. Already the *vaqueros* had scattered and sought cover amongst the rock-covered acclivities of the canyon's sides. One or two even fired rapidly upwards at Ben seeking to drive him back more than to make a direct hit.

Ben decided it was wisest to retreat. He was not prepared to gamble that there were no crack shots amongst the many men Gonzalez had brought with him. He did not rise to his feet until he was sure he could not be seen from below. He was left without a choice now. He had to lure them to the mine and get them inside. He reminded himself that this bunch of cut-throats would watch him burn alive without a qualm. The reminder helped stiffen his resolve. Considerably.

Manolito shot Gonzalez' thrashing horse lest a hoof should strike Gonzalez. He'd been right: they had ridden into an ambush.

'Stay still, *patron*,' Manolito yelled, 'until we are sure he is gone.'

'I want him alive. I want him alive. Do you hear me, damn you!' Gonzalez yelled. Blood from his horse spattered his clothes. He was shaking. It had been close. Only his natural skill and quick wits had saved him.

Manolito decided to ignore the command. Their quarry had proved himself an excellent distance shooter. Had Gonzalez' horse not stumbled, the gringo would have taken off Gonzalez' head. Manolito did not intend to risk his own. He also was an excellent shot. He smiled grimly and yelled out an order. 'Go,' he concluded. 'Or I will kill you myself!'

A narrow, twisted path ran upwards

towards the canyon's rim, a goat path no doubt, but for two men it would not be an impossible feat. When the gringo tried to shoot the two men racing for the path, Manolito would have him. He was confident he could take off the gringo's head.

The two raced desperately for the path, bending low, weaving and doubtless praying. Manolito's finger tightened upon the trigger. Sweat beaded his brow. 'Show yourself, devil, show yourself,' he muttered.

No one showed himself.

Nothing happened.

The two sacrificial goats reached the path and ascended to the rim safely. Shouts from above announced the gringo had departed.

'He's in retreat,' Gonzalez yelled triumphantly as he rose to his feet. 'We have him. We have driven him back to the mine.'

In his haste to commence the manhunt, Gonzalez had not packed clean clothing. His blood-spattered suit was already attracting flies. He swore and batted them, presenting an excellent target for the gringo had he still been around.

Fortunately for Gonzalez the man was indeed gone.

'We can track him from the top,' Manolito announced, seeing Gonzalez was too busy with the flies. 'But we must take the longer route. This way is too dangerous for horses.' They would leave a man behind. The *patron* was in need of a horse.

Manolito held back, always managing to stay just behind Gonzalez' bulk until they reached a spot he deemed climbable. Dismounting, Manolito took the lead. Gonzalez could not be trusted not to slip and take men down with him. The youngest and least able of the company Manolito put at the rear, reasoning that if they must lose a man it made sense to lose the one least needed.

They began to climb upwards, the sun a hot ball in the sky, the sound of hooves upon shale abnormally loud in the sudden stillness. All perspired freely; all wore grim expressions, all had realized that this was no pleasure outing.

Juan's scream of terror reverberated in the stillness, the canyon walls bouncing back the sounds as horse and man lost their footing upon the shifting sliding shale.

'Keep moving,' Manolito snarled. Gonzalez at least needed no urging. He had not turned his head to look back. As always, Gonzalez thought only of his own safety.

Riding towards the mine, Ben heard the echoing scream of the doomed man. One down and a good many more to go. Damn it, how he wished it was Escorpión who came after him.

★ ★ ★

Amigo overturned a bookcase, the contents scattering. He hurled a glass ashtray at a wall mirror. He was as

185

a man possessed, but eventually he calmed. He saw clearly what had to be done. And for this he would need the help of De Bois. He must seek out the fort commander now and insist that De Bois assist him.

The gringo must wait. And so too would fat Elena Gonzalez. He'd have to get rid of her, of course. If he were to inherit this ranch his fat niece must die. His late father's will was quite specific. In the event of Gonzalez' death, if there were no surviving children, the ranch must go to him, Bernardo.

He smiled cruelly. It would be a pleasure to deal with his niece. She had always irritated him. He'd suffocate her. A doctor could be coerced into saying that her heart had simply stopped. Given the size of her this was reasonable.

He had no doubt about the wisdom of going into San Paulo. No one dared challenge him. This knowledge filled him with a sense of omnipotence. If not god, around here, at least he was king. And it was a good feeling. A lesser man might have chosen to ride into San Paulo with armed men at his back. But he, Amigo, would ride in alone. Just to prove that he could.

He rode through the town without fear and rode up to the fort without concern for his safety. None challenged him. All knew him, especially the soldiers, who knew, of course, that De Bois was Gonzalez' man, his future son-in-law. And they knew that Amigo was half-brother to Gonzalez.

Amigo smiled grimly. De Bois ought to go down on his knees and thank him. After all, he'd be saving De Bois from Elena.

He glanced contemptuously at the two men manning the fortified gate. All they need do was close the gates and he would be trapped, snared. Hurriedly they looked away. Amigo laughed contemptuously. Spurs jangling, expression proud, he made his way to De Bois's quarters.

A girl in a tawdry orange gown

bumped into him on her way out of the commander's quarters. A blow from his fist sent her sprawling and a booted foot to her posterior sent her on her way.

Picking up her skirt and none-too-clean petticoat, she ran bare-footed for the gates. And there, to his surprise, remonstrated with the soldiers. They practically threw her out. Slow anger burned inside Amigo as he began to realize she'd been urging the guards to apprehend or kill him. When he had time, when he had taken care of more important matters, he would turn his attention to her. He had not looked at her face, but he would remember the bright orange dress.

De Bois, to Amigo's disgust, lay upon his unmade bed, partly dressed, unconscious, stinking of whiskey, a bottle still clutched in his hand. Empty bottles lay beside the bed.

'Wake up, De Bois.' He gripped the commander's shoulder.

'Bastard,' De Bois grunted, eyes still

closed. 'You damn bastard, Ben Crow. Rot in hell.'

Amigo's eyes narrowed. Who was this crow? He stared hard at De Bois. He needed answers. Who came to hunt him down? How many and, more importantly, when? De Bois might be drunk but he was not unrouseable.

Pain. Pain would arouse the sot. And pain would clear addled wits. Pain would make De Bois listen and it would make him understand and agree to what had to be done.

With a feral smile, Amigo lit an oil lamp. He watched the small flickering flame with fascination. One could imagine it was alive, alive and waiting . . .

De Bois grunted and the sound brought Amigo's mind back to the task in hand. Untying his bandanna, he used it to gag De Bois. Very necessary, for De Bois's howl would bring the troopers running. Amigo propped the slack form up against the pillows. The fool did not even stir or open one eye.

Reaching downwards, Amigo drew a long thin blade from a sheath especially incorporated in his handmade boots. Eyes glinting, he held the tip of the blade in the flames. Just a touch, just a touch with the blade below De Bois's ear and he would have De Bois's attention and co-operation.

Glowing blade in one hand, Amigo used his right hand to catch hold of De Bois's curling hair. He jerked the head upwards and holding the head so pressed the tip of his blade to the spot just behind the ear.

De Bois's eyes opened. In fact they almost popped out of his eye sockets. Feet thrashed. Gargling sounds came from behind the gag.

Reluctantly, Amigo withdrew his blade but made sure that it was held just before De Bois's eyes.

'Now,' he hissed, 'now tell me of this man who troubles your dreams; tell me about Ben Crow.'

# 10

Gonzales gave a shout of triumph when he spotted the bloodstains leading into the mine. 'We have him now,' he yelled. 'The gringo is cornered.'

Manolito was not so sure. And said so, pointing out that the first sign of blood was here and nowhere else.

Gonzalez sent two men into the mine to investigate. They yelled back the cage was down and the man must have descended. Gonzalez was aware that the men were looking to him for leadership.

'We will leave him to die!' he announced. 'Let him rot in the darkness.'

A wizened *vaquero* laughed. 'But suppose he does not die. There are other ways that lead out, narrow tunnels built for such a purpose.' He spat. 'Your brother would not have left this man. This enemy who strikes, this . . . '

'Enough,' Gonzalez roared. 'I am not my brother.'

'No. There can only be one Amigo.'

'A man on foot would not get far.' Manolito moistened his lips. 'We have his horse. Even if he finds a way out thirst and hunger will take him.'

'You are a coward, Manolito. You fear the spirits . . . '

That was as far as the old man got. With a yell, Manolito reached for his pistol. He shot old Pepe through the chest. 'No man calls me a coward.'

'Manolito, take some of the men down with you and flush him out,' Gonzalez ordered. 'Take him alive and we will roast him over a slow fire. You, lay Pepe some distance away amongst the rocks.' He glared at Manolito. 'Your hasty temper ensures we must all endure the smell of putrifying flesh.'

Manolito rubbed his stubbled chin. Anger simmered within him. Gonzalez was a coward. A yellow belly. He feared the mine as did they all.

To Gonzalez' surprise Manolito's scowl was replaced by an ingratiating grin. 'If you do not fear this place of the silent death, *patron*, then neither do I. If you will lead, I will follow.'

A long silence followed. Gonzalez' face darkened. A muscle beneath his eye twitched. He saw through Manolito's ploy. Manolito was gambling that he would not choose to lead them into the mine. He'd been backed into a corner. If he did not lead them he would declare himself coward. There was no way out.

'I will lead you.' One day soon upon their return Manolito would disappear. Gonzalez would arrange it. He'd have a word with his brother. He frowned. Amigo could deal with Manolito before he disappeared. But now he needed the man.

Manolito nodded. He crossed himself.

Gonzalez attempted to smile. 'We will find no ghosts below. All that awaits us is the wounded gringo. Cornered like a rat. He knows the fate that awaits him.'

Ben squatted in the darkness, waiting. They did not come down immediately so perhaps there was some discussion about what to do. They could simply leave, just assume it wasn't worth their time and effort as he was bound to perish anyway. However, Ben was gambling that Gonzalez' desire to take him alive would overrule common sense.

His plan was simple. He would lead them into the mine and then whilst they blundered around in darkness he intended to leave by one of the minor tunnels. He'd return to the main entrance and wait. When they re-emerged disorientated and blinded by the sunlight he would gun them down one by one. With luck maybe the roof would fall in upon the bunch of them, the timber was rotted through and through. He'd had a few uneasy moments himself whilst he'd been exploring and familiarizing himself with the place.

He'd discounted bringing the roof down whilst the bastards were stumbling around. It was too risky as he might bring the roof down upon himself. His luck would not hold indefinitely that was for sure.

He heard the sound of the cage being wound up. That could only mean they were coming down after him. The cage began to descend with much creaking and a lot of profanity.

Hell, all he had to do was to kill the men left up top and the rest of them would be marooned down here stumbling around in the blackness. Sooner or later the oil lamps would be spent. They would never get out then. He didn't even have to shoot the bastards himself.

The cage went up once more and then descended again. He could see them now although they could not see him. Gonzalez held one of the lanterns. It occurred to Ben that he and

Gonzalez, each bent upon destroying the other, would never come closer than this. They would never eye each other face to face. Gonzalez would die none the wiser. Unlike many, Ben did not feel a need to talk, but he did feel a need to groan by way of encouragement, just to start Gonzalez and his men off in the right direction.

'Listen!' Gonzalez ordered.

Smiling grimly, Ben groaned again. He groaned even louder this time and tossed a stone into the tunnel.

'We've got him. Do you hear me, gringo? I'm going to roast you over a fire, head down. How do you like that idea?'

Ben began to move. His boot hit against a long discarded pickaxe. The implement fell with a clatter. His hands skimmed over the rough surface of the wall. He counted his steps knowing just how many steps he must take before he reached the narrow, branching side tunnel, his escape route.

Manolito held his lantern close to the

rocky floor. 'There should be blood to guide us. I see no blood. This wounded man moves quickly.'

Gonzalez ignored his head man. He urged the others on promising a substantial bonus for the first man to see the gringo and an even higher bonus for the man who brought him down.

Ben located the tunnel. With relief he turned into it having first to go down upon his hands and knees. He kept his head down knowing that to raise it risked a hard bump. As suddenly as it had narrowed, the tunnel expanded. Ben was able to stand now, although the width of the tunnel was such that a stouter man, such as Gonzalez, would not have got through.

The tunnel forked. Ben chose the left fork knowing that this one actually led back to the surface. He wondered how long it would be before Gonzalez who would have gone blundering on ahead would realize Ben was no longer fleeing before him. How long would it be before Gonzalez tried to turn back? The main tunnel twisted and turned and forked. It would be very easy for the hunting party to lose all sense of direction.

'Stop!' Manolito held up his hand. 'We have lost him, *patron*.' He was convinced the gringo was no longer ahead of them.

The darkness pressed in upon them and the only sound was the sound of their laboured breathing. Manolito could smell their fear. They were men who belonged in the saddle, not below ground stumbling in darkness.

'The man is wounded. He cannot be far ahead,' Gonzalez persisted.

'He is not wounded. The blood was but a trick. He wanted us to follow him down into the depth of hell. And now he has slipped away down one of the side tunnels. As he must have intended all along.'

'I am not a fool,' Gonzalez snapped. 'The man did not buy further explosives before leaving San Paulo. Every place of sale was checked. He came to this place on impulse. His sole purpose in returning to San Paulo was to send a telegraph.'

'Ah yes, the telegraph. It will cause much trouble I think.' Manolito's voice was grim. 'We will go back now, *patron*. We cannot proceed further. To do so would be confusing. Nor will our lamps last indefinitely.'

'Very well. You may lead us back.' Gonzalez managed to sound as though he were conveying a favour. In reality, he was making sure that if they could not so easily retrace their footsteps, the blame would fall upon Manolito and not upon himself.

'I will do my utmost, *patron*,' Manolito sneered, knowing the task was beyond Gonzalez. He fought to conquer his fear. He was uncertain as to whether he could lead them back. If there was trouble Gonzalez would pay. He should never have brought them down here. Gonzalez had been a fool to lead them into this trap.

Ben found his way to the surface without difficulty. He had no fears that Gonzalez was close upon his heels. He knocked out the rotting wood shoring up the makeshift tunnel. Dirt showered down closing the exit. He visited each of the other two tunnels in turn and likewise rendered them useless, acknowledging that whilst he'd been crawling out the roof could have come down upon him at any time.

That done, crouching low and using the rocks as cover, he made his way back to the main entrance his eyes searching for the two men assigned to wind the cage and keep vigil. They were easily spotted lying a little way from the cage opening. Left to their own devices they had opened a bottle of cheap wine and lay snoring.

He'd never shot a sleeping man and he was not going to start now not even with these two. Forty-five drawn, he carefully disarmed the two ready to shoot if either one of them so much as twitched. But the two snored on.

Ben booted the nearest one. The man came awake with a grunt and a curse. He fell silent, however, when he found himself staring into the mouth of Ben's .45.

'Do not kill me I beg you,' he babbled. 'I have a wife and four children.'

'Do you now. Wake up your pard,' Ben rejoined unimpressed. 'And then get that damn cage wound pronto.' His finger tightened on the trigger. 'Don't even twitch. I don't need an excuse to blast you bastards.'

As he'd expected, no one voiced any argument. The two were pathetically eager to obey. He had no reason to show these two mercy save one, and that was that he had not yet become a ruthless killing machine. He was better than the Gonzalezes and Amigos of this world, not to mention scum like Edward Bacon and his block-headed foreman, Meaks.

The cage rewound, Ben glared at the two hirelings. What to do with them posed a problem, one that he ought to have considered before he decided not to despatch them. Bound, both would die of thirst and starvation. Freed, they'd be quick to haul up the cage and Gonzalez. Toting them along with him was an idea he did not care for much either. They'd slow him considerably. And there was always the chance they'd have an opportunity to jump him.

He was undecided. The dark part of his nature urged him to blast them and have done with it. They were his enemies out to get him but even so . . . Ben decided to sleep on it. Dusk was falling. He had to camp here. Tomorrow, when daylight broke, he'd decide. Meantime, hog-tied the two could sweat it out. They would find it a long night pondering their fate.

Under his watchful eye one of them tied up the other. And then Ben hog-tied the remaining man, all the while listening for Gonzalez and company — assuming that the polecats eventually made it back to the cage.

Either the Lord or the Devil was with him. Manolito succeeded in leading them back to the shaft, but not before he'd taken two wrong turnings and had been forced to retrace his steps. Each time he'd been sick with fear that he would fail to find the shaft.

Gonzalez lumbered along at his heel, cannoning into Manolito each time Manolito hesitated. Each time Manolito glanced around the terrified eyes of the crew looked back at him. The stench of fear increased. And then, just as the oil lamps flickered and dimmed, Gonzalez saw the shaft.

'You old woman, Manolito,' he yelled. 'You worry for nothing. Didn't I tell you we'd get back. Here we are and not a man lost.'

'Much good will it do us.' Manolito rounded on his boss. 'The cage is gone. The gringo is behind this.' He raised his voice. 'Gringo, can you hear me?'

Shouts answered him. Not the gringo, but the two worthless dogs Gonzalez had left on guard. They yelled back that the gringo had them and that they were bound and helpless.

Ben, who had been dozing, awoke with a string of curses. Stumbling to his feet, he kicked out at the forms in the darkness. His boot tip connected with flesh.

'Shut up,' he rasped. 'Shut up or I'll cut out your goddamn tongues. I'll . . . ' He delivered a few more kicks for good measure and then settled down again choosing to ignore whoever was yelling that he wished to speak with the gringo.

The thought of Gonzalez deep below ground in stifling darkness was a pleasant thought. It was justice. Gonzalez had condemned many men to such a fate. And he'd watched men burn, those who had tried to escape from the hell of the Elena Gonzalez Mine.

'Shut up, Manolito,' Gonzalez hissed. He raised his voice. 'Name your price, gringo. How much do you want to send down the cage?'

Ben ignored the lunatic.

'I have a candle, *patron*.'

'Light it,' Gonzalez ordered.

'No. Save it,' Manolito counter-manded. 'Tomorrow, before he leaves, the gringo will make contact. He will wish to gloat, to taunt . . . ' And perhaps the man could be reasoned with.

As far as Manolito was concerned this was not a personal vendetta. He and the men were here because the man who paid their wages had brought them here. The gringo's quarrel was with Gonzalez not with honest, hardworking men.

Ben came awake as the blackness of night gave way to the greyness of dawn. Even a bug-infested hotel room was preferable to hard ground, he reflected sourly. Life had been a darn sight more comfortable and simpler when he'd been a mere gambler.

He became aware that one of the bastards below was yelling again.

'Gringo,' he yelled. 'Are you there?'

'He is here,' one of the bound men

responded and then shut up as Ben rose to his feet.

'We have no quarrel with you, gringo,' Manolito yelled desperately. 'We wish you no harm. We mean you no harm. We are simple men trying to provide for our women and children. For mercy's sake, gringo, you cannot leave us here to die like rats.' There was a pause. 'We will prove that we mean you no harm,' the voice yelled desperately.

'Oh yeah,' Ben mumbled, deciding to brew coffee.

'Light the candle,' Manolito screeched. 'Light it I say. Soon the man will ride away.'

The candle was lit.

'Manolito, what is your plan?' Gonzalez asked.

Manolito picked up a discarded pickaxe. 'I have no plan, *patron*. But I know what must be done. The gringo must be convinced. Only then will he spare us.'

'Convinced!' Gonzalez failed to

understand. 'How?'

'Like this.' Manolito swung the pickaxe and brought Gonzalez down. 'Like this. It is the only way.' He raised the pickaxe again. 'Help me, you dogs.'

Ben heard the long drawn-out howl. And then there were a good many howls, loud at first but then dying down as the howler weakened. There were cries for mercy interposed with the howls of pain. At the end, the man, and it was Gonzalez, was begging.

Following Manolito's lead the terrified men laid into Gonzalez with picks and shovels and anything they could find. For a moment they became as a pack of wild dogs as they struck the man responsible for their predicament.

'Let down the cage, *señor*,' Manolito yelled desperately. 'Let me show you the proof of our good intention.'

Ben had a good idea what he was going to see. He let down the cage. From the top of the shaft he could peer down. When the cage ascended he'd be able to see through the open roof. If there was anyone alive in the cage he'd send the cage plunging back and that would be an end of it.

What came up was unrecognizable. He knew he was viewing the remains of Gonzalez. His appetite had deserted him. Hell, those fear-crazed bastards had set to work with a vengeance.

Still, despite what they had done, he did not trust the bastards below. But with Gonzalez now gone he did not feel that his conscience would allow him to leave them entombed. He'd give them a chance to make it back. But they must travel on foot. He was not so foolish as to leave them their horses.

The Elena Gonzalez Mine itself still remained. But Gonzalez, the force behind the mine, was gone. Ben sighed. He still had Amigo to deal with. And the hell of it was that he did not know how he was going to deal with Amigo. True, life was going to be a great deal more difficult for Amigo with Gonzalez gone and outsiders showing an interest in his activities.

* * *

Amigo laughed until his sides hurt from laughing. He was the one who had brought the gringo here. Gonzalez was as nothing to the gringo. It was he the gringo sought.

The man could only be Miss Dorothy's lover. Although it was hard to imagine Miss Dorothy loving anyone or being loved. Doubtless the man was as crazy as Miss Dorothy. This gambler, this gentleman who no doubt considered himself superior to a humble Mexican.

'All along you have known of this man and yet you gave no warning,' he accused De Bois. He smiled unpleasantly. 'Well, now at least I know how to trap him. I must give him time, of course, time to deal with my stupid brother, time to return from the old mine. He shall have time and then I shall set my trap.'

'What trap?' De Bois asked without understanding.

'Why, I shall let it be known,' Amigo smiled, 'that I intend to burn Miss Dorothy. To save her he must come to me. But first, De Bois my good friend, we must deal with your comrade Hernandez. We have time I think.'

# 11

De Bois poured cold water over his aching head. He was alone. The monster had gone.

It could not be done. He could not help Amigo ambush Hernandez. It was far too risky; by helping to destroy Hernandez he would be helping to destroy himself. Amigo, of course, could not see this and if he did he did not care. De Bois did not give a damn about Hernandez, he cared that it could not be done secretly. Afterwards, doubtless Amigo planned to slip away leaving De Bois up on a charge.

And if Amigo thought Crow would sacrifice himself to save Miss Dorothy the man really was crazy.

Just what the hell he was going to do to get himself out of this mess De Bois did not know.

Meaks knew that something was wrong. One day the prisoners were being worked until none of them could stand in an attempt to get the mine operational again, the next they were kept locked in their prison sheds. And the day after that. Food and water were grudgingly distributed and that was all.

The stifling sheds were hell but preferable to the hell which awaited below ground. Tension grew amongst the prisoners as they waited for something to happen.

De Bois saw the court martial looming before him. In his mind he planned his defence. His only crime, he would plead disarmingly, would be to fall deeply in love with Elena Gonzalez. Of course, if the court were to see Elena they would find that statement hard to believe, but what else could he do but plead she was his only connection with the rancher Gonzalez?

Gonzalez should have had better sense than to go into the hills in pursuit of Crow. The man was an armchair rancher who paid others to do his dirty work. He was no manhunter and was a fool to attempt it. Knowing Crow, De Bois was convinced Gonzalez was not going to return. And if Gonzalez was not going to return that left De Bois free to take certain steps which he could use as his defence.

One of the accusations he might face was that he had known all along what was going on out at the Elena Gonzalez Mine. That he'd been a party to slavery. That he'd known all along drifters and saddle-bums and any luckless peon who displeased Gonzalez was shipped out to the mine never to be seen again. It followed, therefore, to prove his innocence in that respect, he must remedy the situation out at the mine.

And there was only one way to do that.

As for his fiancée, the girl was a

fool. Now she had shut herself away in a convent whilst she considered her future. Even Amigo had not been allowed in to speak with his niece. De Bois failed to see why this had caused the bandit such rage.

Having decided to lead his troops against the mine, De Bois dressed with great care. He kicked his orderly because his boots were not polished to his satisfaction and then strode out to address the assembled troop.

He sensed their unease. Rumour had spread that they rode to winkle out and destroy the bandit Amigo. However, hand resting upon the hilt of his sword, he swiftly dispersed their fears on that score. They looked a good deal happier once he had finished speaking, every word a lie, of course, but no one was going to argue with him.

Leading his men out of San Paulo, De Bois put the blame for what he must do squarely on Crow's shoulders. The so-called gentleman gambler had set a stone rolling which was fast turning into a landslide. No one could call a halt.

★ ★ ★

Only after he had put many miles between himself and the old mine did Ben realize what a fool he had been. With hindsight, now that it was too late to do anything about matters, he could see his mistake.

For a brief time, Gonzalez and his hirelings had been at his mercy. They would have done anything to get out of the mine. Also Ben knew he could have broken any one of them, especially Gonzalez. It followed that Gonzalez and a few of the others knew the way to Amigo's camp. Ben should have had a map drawn.

He could not storm the outlaws' camp but the soldiers coming in to aid De Bois could. All Ben would have needed to do was to slip into the camp before the attack; his objective to keep Miss Dorothy safe and let the

215

army deal with the outlaw band.

Alone, Ben could handle Amigo. If Amigo would settle things man to man. But Ben was not fool enough to believe that Amigo would battle alone.

Not having a plan or even an idea, Ben found himself riding back towards San Paulo. There must be someone in that town who could provide him with a map. It was the key he needed and he'd do whatever was necessary to get that map drawn. He could not be merciful again, not if he wanted to come out of this alive. Rescuing Miss Dorothy was no longer the important issue here. The important issue was stopping the crazy man-burner before he could claim any more victims.

From a distant ridge overlooking the town, Ben observed the army column riding out. He recognized the lead man even from a distance. And he was puzzled as to where they might be going. Surely De Bois was not riding against Amigo?

After a moment's thought Ben

dismissed the idea. De Bois was not suicidal. In fact, the man had a strong sense of self-preservation. Puzzled, Ben decided to tag along behind the column. He'd eat their dust but he didn't care.

De Bois had always put Ben in mind of one of the toy soldiers he'd had as a child. Instinct told men that De Bois had never done any real soldiering, never seen action, family connections had got him this posting.

His disbelief grew as it became pretty clear that the column could only be heading for the Elena Gonzalez Mine. They rode at a steady pace obviously not in a hurry to reach their destination. As De Bois did not hesitate, it was pretty clear the man was familiar with the route.

A short distance from the mine, but out of sight of the place, De Bois brought the column to a halt. Turning to face his men he delivered a morale-boosting speech concluding with the words that as they were dealing with desperate men no quarter need be given.

They all understood. There was an air of excitement amongst them now, excitement and anticipation. He felt the same way himself. His first skirmish and he did not feel fear.

And nor should you, an inner voice jibed. Those bastards Gonzalez pays to run his mine are not going to put up much of a fight. De Bois wanted none left alive, no one who might accuse him of having visited once before as a guest of Gonzalez. Of necessity, De Bois decided he must risk himself. He did not like the idea, but it must be done. He must ensure that his men could sweep down into the mine without hindrance.

Leaving his men concealed, De Bois, with his bugler at his side, rode confidently down towards the mine. He was spotted, of course, but the two or three men lounging around evinced no sign of alarm for they knew him as Gonzalez' man. Indeed, they obligingly pushed the gate wide open to afford him passage.

As De Bois rode through the gate a rider passed him. De Bois hesitated and the man passed on.

'Have you news of Gonzalez?' the guard enquired. He squinted up at De Bois clearly thinking De Bois brought news.

'I have reason to believe that men are being held here against their will. Enslaved and forced to work this mine. What say you!'

The guard was not afforded a chance to respond. Drawing his sword, De Bois brought the blade swishing viciously downwards as the bugler sounded the attack.

The troop swept down immediately; swords drawn, their intention clear. Ben topped the ridge. He watched the ensuing carnage as men were hacked to pieces or shot.

To the left of the mine; a rider streaked away from the place, riding as though the Devil were after him.

Not that any of the troopers had sought to give pursuit. Clearly De Bois was unconcerned with keeping this a secret. Indeed, it was a public display.

Ben could envisage De Bois's dispatch. Rumour had reached him. He had investigated. The slave labourers had been released. No mention would be made of the men he had ordered slaughtered.

It occurred to Ben he'd best get riding. The one who had escaped might possibly head for Amigo's lair. Who else was there for him to report to? Ben knew he had to catch the escaping man. With luck he'd have his map.

When the prison sheds were opened, the stench was overpowering. Thin, stick figures stumbled out. They grovelled their thanks before De Bois. Two even clutched his boots.

De Bois delivered his speech. Wagons would be brought to transport them into San Paulo. Once in San Paulo each man could purchase a stage ticket to whatever destination he chose. Or alternatively he might purchase a horse and supplies. The said ticket or horse to be charged to Gonzalez. Beggars were frowned upon in San Paulo so it was best that each man moved on as quickly as was possible.

Meaks watched the grovelling with disgust. He kept his head down not turning his eyes to look at the fancy Mexican who'd come to their salvation, and was now so keen to see them gone. Meaks climbed into a cart along with the others, unnoticed, just another saddle-bum.

As the cart trundled out, Meaks glanced at the bodies scattered around. No one as far as he could see had been left alive. Food was being taken also, to be distributed once they reached the outskirts of San Paulo.

Meaks thinned his lips. He would not be moving out. He was going after Miss Dorothy. Maybe he'd even run into Crow. Meaks guessed he'd better look out. Crow was liable to shoot first and think about it afterwards.

As the convoy rode into San Paulo, Meaks observed that the Mexican commander's return was not greeted with a rousing cheer. A good many of those who had turned out to watch looked plainly apprehensive. Reluctantly, a black-garbed cleric congratulated De Bois, seemed to think better of it and then scurried away.

This lack of enthusiasm made Meaks all the more determined to keep his mouth shut and ears open. There was no help to be got willingly from these people.

To Meaks's surprise, De Bois took the sick man who lay in one of the wagons to the fort. This surprised Meaks for it would have been more in keeping with the Mexican's character simply to have tipped the sick man out and leave him lying upon the street.

★ ★ ★

Amigo took great pleasure in informing Miss Dorothy that he intended to burn her unless a certain *hombre* called Ben Crow turned up to burn in her place.

To his surprise, Miss Dorothy babbled that if Benjamin were to hasten to her side he would be invisible for the dead could not walk amongst the living observed. It soon became clear that Miss Dorothy had memorized long tracts of the Bible for she began to quote from it now. Defeated, his enjoyment soured, he left her alone.

Ben had got as near to Amigo's camp as it was safe to venture. He lay on a low hill overlooking a shallow valley. At the far side of the valley, towering rocks guarded and shielded the camp. Had he not been aware of its existence he would not have first spotted the narrow cleft in the rocks. Beyond the cleft lay the camp of Amigo.

Ben had decided the best thing to do was watch the camp. Sooner or later word would reach the bandit leader that troops had arrived in San Paulo. Ben needed to know how Amigo would react. There was a chance he would simply pack up camp and move on with Miss Dorothy in tow. Or he might simply kill her.

Time passed slowly during his watch. Patience was not one of his strong points. He hated inactivity, but he could not, he kept reminding himself, afford to make a mistake because that mistake might be his last. The hell of it was he could not come up with any kind of workable plan. And so he watched.

The rider streaked across the valley quirting his flagging horse. Clearly the man had ridden his horse practically into the ground. Ben had a hunch that his time of inactivity would be coming to an end. He guessed the back-up troops if not on their way, were at least within the vicinity of San Paulo.

The rider brought his horse to a halt before the opening, dismounted and raised his hands to his mouth. Ben had ascertained from the guard he had taken that four owl hoots was the signal. That information had saved the guard's life. There was no way Ben with his damaged vocal chords could hoot like an owl. He had, therefore, been forced to tote the guard along.

Hell, he wished he was a fly upon the wall when the messenger arrived.

Amigo's lookout man raced for the white stone house. 'Amigo, they are coming,' he yelled. 'They are within a day's march of San Paulo.'

Amigo, cigar in his mouth, appeared in the door-way.

'Calm yourself,' he ordered. 'All will be well.'

'De Bois has destroyed the Elena Gonzalez Mine. He has freed the captives and slaughtered the guards.'

Amigo nodded. 'De Bois will pay for his presumption. Later. For now we need him.' Gonzalez, most certainly would not be returning. The man Crow had killed his brother. And now Crow, most annoyingly, had dropped out of sight. He had not returned to San Paulo. Amigo had planted three of his men in town to watch for Crow and report.

Amigo smiled. 'It is time to deal with Hernandez.'

'Shall we burn him?'

'Unfortunately no. He must be dealt with quickly and at one stroke. He and his men must perish together. Now, rouse the camp. We ride immediately. We have much to do!'

Ben smiled grimly. The lead rider wore a striking yellow jacket. The man could only be Amigo, out to draw attention to himself. Confident that no bullet would find him. Unfortunately, the man was too distant for Ben to attempt a shot. And it looked as if Amigo was taking most of his men with him. 'Hell,' Ben muttered. It was clear this bastard rode with his own private army. It was, therefore, not surprising De Bois had not wanted to tangle with him.

Ben waited until Amigo and his men were no longer even a dust cloud. It was now, Ben had decided. He had to go in now. If Miss Dorothy were alive he'd get her out.

He booted his prisoner lying hog-tied, gagged and terrified. 'It's time you made yourself useful. After that you can go to the devil. You'll have betrayed Amigo and that man accepts no excuses. Whatever you do or say he'll roast you.'

With Miss Dorothy in tow Ben would become the hunted. That crazy bastard would pick up his trail and follow him. Even over the border they would not be safe. Until Amigo was planted Ben would forever be looking over his shoulder, forever anticipating the slug or knife which would bury itself in his flesh. Hell, he wasn't happy. Miss Dorothy slowing him down might well be the death of him second time around.

'We'll change clothes,' Ben ordered. 'I'll pretend to be bringing you in. Keep your hat pulled down low. Don't even think of saving the bastard who has been left as lookout.'

Leaving the Mexican's horse concealed, Ben decided to lead his prisoner towards the cleft. He fashioned a rope noose and placed it round the captive's neck and loosely bound the man's wrists in front of him just for show. He still might need the man to hoot. He intended to keep his word and let the varmint go.

They descended and crossed the valley without being challenged. Reaching the narrow entrance, the Mexican cupped his hands to his mouth and hooted. Sweat dampened the back of Ben's shirt. It was hotter than hell. Pretty soon hell would be welcoming Amigo's man or men. Ben did not know how many he'd have to kill.

The lookout man appeared. There was a grin upon his face. 'You have the gringo!'

He might have said more, but Ben's blade buried itself in his throat. He went down with a gurgle, blood gushing, accusing eyes staring at Ben.

'*Señor!*'

Ben rounded on his captive. 'Cut yourself free and get before I decide to plant you. Leave the knife.' He watched whilst the prisoner freed himself and then ran stumbling towards the hill and his horse.

Ben rode gingerly through the cleft. To his surprise the tunnel between the towering rock faces immediately widened. Amigo had chosen a fine hideout for himself, Ben reflected. But the bandit leader had grown complacent and careless. Too many outsiders knew the location of the hideout. Amigo had merely relied on fear of burning to keep them silent. Fear of what Ben had promised to do had loosened the captive's tongue.

Despite the seriousness of his situation, Ben grinned. It helped to have an inventive imagination, but it irked that the Mexican had believed him, believed him to be as bad as Amigo.

'What news do you bring?' The second man stepped out from amongst the acclivities. The fool had played

229

right into Ben's hands.

Ben beckoned.

The fool approached.

Slipping his feet free of the stirrups Ben launched himself at the unsuspecting Mexican. They fought silently, the Mexican trying to reach for his pistol. Ben snapped the man's neck, a trick Linelli had taught him which he had not so far had occasion to use.

He scowled. He was tempted to snap Miss Dorothy's scrawny neck, but it was a temptation he must resist.

No one challenged him as he rode into the camp. Hardly surprising because all he saw were women and a few children. It was easy to spot Amigo's place, the large, white stone house complete with porch which stood out amongst the shacks the men used. Ben simply tethered his horse before the porch, opened the door which was unlocked and clumped in as though he had every right to be there.

'Miss Dorothy!' he croaked. 'Miss Dorothy.' As he called he opened doors to the right and left of the long corridor, slamming them hard to attract her attention.

'Here, I am here!'

Ben simply turned the key and shoved the heavy wooden door open forcefully. Miss Dorothy's eyes stared at him wildly.

'But they hanged you!'

'No they didn't, Miss Dorothy. The Devil looks after his own.' He paused. 'I'm here to save you,' he informed her, lest she think he was there to snap her neck which was what she deserved.

'Behind you,' she screeched.

# 12

Ben spun round, his hand reaching for his gun. There wasn't time to think, the need to save himself was paramount. He couldn't afford to make the mistake of underestimating a woman again. He'd never seen Miss Dorothy as a threat and look where that had got him? On the end of a rope that was where.

Amigo's sister Maria stood behind him, her face twisted with hate. In her raised hand the girl held a long-bladed knife. With a screech she lunged forward. Ben's finger squeezed the trigger of his levelled Colt .45. As the gun roared the girl was almost upon him. Ben caught her as she fell, her upturned face looking straight towards him as the light began to fade from her eyes.

Ben cursed savagely. He'd never

wanted this to happen no matter that she was the monster's sister and that she had condemned many men to toil and die underground. The blood from the girl stained his clothing. He owed his life to Miss Dorothy's screech of warning he realized dully.

'That girl was as rotten as her brother,' Miss Dorothy declared. 'You can take my word for it.' She grabbed Ben's sleeve. 'Hurry. We have to get out of here. One of those women will be riding after Amigo. She'll alert him. Yes, indeed.'

Ben let Maria's dead body slide to the ground.

'I know how to open his safe. The braggart revealed the combination.'

Ben guessed that was not all Amigo had revealed. He felt his ears turn red. Certain things were never mentioned.

'I'll make amends for what I did,' Miss Dorothy babbled. 'He'll hunt us whether we take the money or not. And,' she added, 'he has made clear his intention to burn me.'

'Hell!' Ben's protests died away. They might as well take the money then. They'd need it. Him and Miss Dorothy. Not that he intended staying around Miss Dorothy a moment longer than was necessary.

Amigo's safe was behind a picture of the bandit leader. Without hesitation, Miss Dorothy opened the safe and shovelled the contents into a faded valise, not to mention two gunny sacks.

'Get outside, Benjamin. I'll be but a moment.'

'Well, mind you are,' he snapped, wondering what kind of welcome awaited them outside.

The women and children left behind had not approached the house but stood some distance away. One, Ben observed, toted a rifle. 'Put that damn weapon down,' he yelled, sweat beading his brow. The corral was open which meant one of them had taken off after Amigo.

Goddamnit, she was raising the rifle.

Ben fired. The woman fell to the ground screaming. Blood stained her skirt for he had fired at a leg hindered, of course, by her skirts and petticoats, just hoping to do minimum damage.

The whole bunch of them took off screaming and wailing. 'Hell!' Ben roared, he'd never envisaged having to shoot women.

Miss Dorothy appeared holding an empty can.

'What the hell!'

She ignored him; bending, she lit a match.

Ben grabbed her and yanked her off the porch fearful that her own clothing would catch light. 'Goddamnit woman, mount up,' he rasped, as the horses plunged in terror. He thrust her up into the saddle. She clutched the pommel helplessly. Ben mounted, grabbed Miss Dorothy's reins and dug in his heels. They left at the gallop.

'Murderer! Assassin!'

He smiled bitterly. That those crazy women should yell accusations was beyond belief. He guessed Miss Dorothy would have replied with a few choice remarks of her own if she had not been hanging on for dear life. He slowed the horses as they approached the exit. Here they were vulnerable, but he guessed it would not have occurred to the woman who had taken off to try and ambush them. Nevertheless, his eyes were wary.

'What are we going to do?' Miss Dorothy all but wailed as they came out of the cleft.

'Damned if I know, Miss Dorothy, damned if I know,' Ben rejoined. 'Maybe we can join up with the soldiers on their way to deal with Amigo. Or maybe not. Last thing we want to do is run into that bastard.' He paused. 'One thing is for sure: we have to know he is dead. He'll follow us both wherever we go. Alone or separated he'll hunt us down.'

\* \* \*

Whatever happened De Bois had decided he was not going to be accused of conspiring with the bandit Amigo to slaughter Hernandez. Of course, if he should refuse, the bandit Amigo was capable of shooting him there and then. The man was quite mad. He never thought of the consequences of his deeds. There was only one thing De Bois could do and he did it. He issued orders that the gates of the fort be barred and that no one be allowed admittance or exit for there was infection within the fort. The sick miner burned with fever. The sick miner had proved useful. De Bois had been about to have the man tipped out of the cart and left when the idea had occurred to him to quarantine the fort.

Meaks, holed up in an alleyway, chewing a hunk of dried bread, so far had not experienced any sign of fever. Hell, he reflected, the folk of San Paulo took some beating. They'd all but chased the luckless bastards from the mine out of town. True, the men had been given horses and meagre supplies, but stones had been thrown and threats made. All because De Bois had quarantined the fort.

Meaks, however, had been overlooked. So here he sat, back resting against an adobe wall, knees bent almost to his chin, watching and waiting. This town was a powder keg.

Meaks was confident that he could force anyone, man or woman, to reveal the location of the bandits' lair. There were ways to break a man and Meaks knew them. His problem was he had to grab the right galoot. He had to grab someone who knew. And as yet he didn't know who to take.

Crow had certainly stirred things up. The identity of Gonzalez' enemy was known now. Word had spread. Everyone spoke of Ben Crow, speculating as to what Crow might be doing now. Meaks himself wished he knew. At the back of his mind was a fear Crow would lose control and kill Miss Dorothy. Most men would, Meaks recognized.

As Amigo rode into town with only two men, Meaks remained unaware of his arrival. He also remained unaware of Amigo's departure.

Amigo rode out of San Paulo his face expressionless. 'Get out of here, you dog,' the terrified conscript had yelled when Amigo had demanded admittance. Most faces were averted, Amigo saw, but there were some who smirked at him. 'The Devil is coming for you, Amigo, and his name is Hernandez,' a derisive voice yelled, the speaker concealed. His eyes gleamed. His lieutenant recognized the mad gleam. He knew what it meant. San Paulo was going to pay.

The band was camped a little distance from San Paulo. They had taken over a grove of trees. Men lounged in the shade and many raised bottles to their lips.

'We have been betrayed.' Amigo regarded his men. 'You may loot the town. De Bois will do nothing to stop you. Kill all that moves. We have no further use for San Paulo.'

'He will follow us. He must.' the lieutenant referred to De Bois.

Amigo nodded. 'He will make a pretence of following us. We will burn De Bois. He is a posturing coward. No one betrays me and lives.'

Meaks heard the shots and the whoops and the cries. He jumped to his feet stifling his first impulse which was to run out of the alley and see what the hell was going on. Drunken drovers riding into town — save no drovers drunk or otherwise had ever ridden into this town.

A man appeared in the mouth of the alleyway. The barber. His white apron stained red. Hands clutched the reddening stain and then the barber keeled over.

'Hell.' Meaks pressed back against the wall. The luckless *hombre* had been belly shot. Meaks did not understand why. But San Paulo was under attack, inconceivably, considering San Paulo enjoyed the protection of an army garrison.

Meaks couldn't think at first. It would be savage and short. He had to play possum. Meaks lurched towards the dead man. He grabbed the body, hauling the man back into the alleyway. Meaks laid the body face down and then crawled beneath the bulky corpse hoping it would look as if two had been shot dead in the alleyway. He pressed his face against the dirt, closed his eyes and prayed as he'd never done before.

Amigo dismounted before the church. He had a score to settle with the black-robed cleric. As a boy he'd been beaten by the priest because he'd been caught stealing from the church. His father had agreed with the priest. To this day Amigo did not know why it was right to steal from all others but not the Church. That had been his father's belief. He kicked open the door and strode into the church. It was cool within, light streaming through the stained-glass windows to puddle the floor. He found the cleric kneeling at the altar. Seizing the fat priest's collar, Amigo simply hauled him out into the square before the church.

The slaughter was over now. Those who had escaped the bullets were being rounded-up to witness Amigo's departing gesture.

'An old woman commands the fort,' Amigo cried. 'Know you all De Bois is a snivelling coward.'

'No,' the priest screamed, eyes riveted upon the stake which had already been set up.

'Who is man enough to stop me?' Amigo yelled. 'Let that man speak.'

No one spoke. Amigo laughed. 'There are no men in San Paulo,' he taunted, 'only women.'

Meaks heard the fearsome screams. He didn't so much as twitch in case someone should look into the alleyway. He could smell the smoke. Another luckless bastard was being torched by the maniac. As the screams rose to a crescendo and then died away, Meaks felt a tear course down his cheeks.

The woman was waiting for Amigo when he led his men back to the grove.

'Aiyee,' she screamed. 'Aiyee, your sister dead and . . . '

He seized her shoulders. 'Who?' he thundered. 'Who?' But he knew the answer. It could only be the elusive gringo. This man Crow. He had come for Miss Dorothy when he'd least been expected.

★ ★ ★

Hernandez sensed at once that something was wrong. San Paulo lay below shimmering in the heat. Overhead the sky was clear and blue, the clouds mere wisps of white. Hernandez could not but help recollect a line from a book he had read once. A good day to die, the words had stayed in his mind ever since.

Not that he had any intention of

dying. Expression grim, he started down towards the town. He was here to do what De Bois could not or would not do. He would rid the countryside of the bandit. He would hang the man and those of his men who survived in the town square before the church, after he'd had them whipped within an inch of their lives. And then Gonzalez who had reportedly sheltered the killer would be brought to trial. Witnesses could easily be found to incriminate the man. Once in Hernandez' care men were quick to say that which Hernandez wanted to hear. Hernandez had been described as self-righteous and ruthless. He was both.

As Hernandez approached, a thin ribbon began to wind itself away from the town. A black ribbon he observed. People walking in single file, heads bowed. Behind them came a cart filled with sacks.

Closer observation revealed them to be bodies wrapped in sacking. The ribbon shuffled forward, turning east towards the cemetery. No one acknowledged Hernandez' presence.

'What happened?' he called. 'What is this?'

Dull eyes were turned towards him. 'Amigo is this,' a man replied. Hernandez saw his cheeks were furrowed with tears.

'Where is De Bois? Where is your priest? How could this happen?' This time no one troubled to respond. Hernandez' lips tightened at the insult, but in the circumstances he could do nothing. He spurred his horse forward galloping down a narrow paved street which led towards the town square and the church. No one blocked his way. Here as elsewhere the place was deserted.

Emerging into the sunlit square, he reined in his horse. Before him, in the centre of the square directly before the church, stood a stake. Hernandez stared at the charred stake and charred bones.

'Sacrilege!' he cried. The bandit had

burnt the priest before his own church. He saw also the open porch door and knew without looking that the bandit had desecrated the church. And the heavens had not opened and struck him down. Hernandez found that thought disturbing.

He clenched his hands tightly. Where was De Bois while this outrage was taking place? That a town in the shadow of an army garrison had been attacked was beyond belief. Truly De Bois had much to answer for. Vowing vengeance, Hernandez galloped towards the fort, his men close behind. This had become more than a routine duty.

★ ★ ★

Amigo stood alone. Never before had he experienced such overwhelming hatred for a man he had not yet seen face to face. Hatred for a man he knew little about; hatred for the gambler, Ben Crow.

His sister Maria, now nothing more

than charred bones, lay at his feet. Although the walls of his house still stood, the interior of his home was a charred ruin. His safe gaped open.

The she-devil had stolen his money and burnt his house before fleeing with Crow. He no longer found Miss Dorothy amusing. He had erred keeping her alive in order to bait her. He ought to have killed her long ago. His lips twisted. Now he had paid for his mistake.

★ ★ ★

Meaks had not galloped wildly in pursuit of the departing outlaw band. An inner voice had warned him that he would be riding into danger. Meaks had accordingly stayed put waiting to see what happened next.

In fact a considerable amount of time passed before De Bois, immaculately dressed, led his troops out to pursue the bandit. Professing outrage, De Bois lingered in the town square supposedly praying for the burnt cleric. Meaks was not fooled. He recognized delaying tactics when he saw them. Cautiously, holding back, Meaks followed on behind the troop. He was aware that this was a mere token pursuit.

It was not long before Meaks determined that the route Amigo had taken passed through country ideal if one wanted to spring an ambush. He wondered De Bois did not see it. Meaks allowed himself to fall back still further.

When the ambush was sprung Meaks was not surprised. He waited hidden amongst the brush. What he saw once the ambush was over did not surprise him either. No one was left alive. Most, Meaks determined were killed immediately. Those who lingered had their throats cut. All were scalped, including De Bois who had taken a fatal wound to the chest. Leaving the dead for the carrion, Meaks resumed his cautious pursuit. The outlaw band was travelling at speed now, moving upwards into the hills.

He guessed he'd find the camp, but not Miss Dorothy. Crow, he reckoned, had got there before him.

* * *

Miss Dorothy's face was grey with tiredness. She bounced up and down, butt thumping against her saddle. Her eyes were glazed. Having her riding alongside him had slowed Crow down considerably. He began to admit now that he could not outdistance the pursuers as long as he had Miss Dorothy with him. But he was damned if he was prepared to leave her.

So what the hell was he going to do, he asked himself yet again? There was no help to be had anywhere. The only galoot crazy enough to stand with him against Amigo was Linelli and he was far distant.

'Leave me,' Miss Dorothy gasped. 'I don't want your death on my conscience a second time.'

Mighty noble of you Miss Dorothy, he thought. 'Never knew you had a conscience, Miss Dorothy,' he joshed. The joke fell flat. She burst into tears. 'I'm not leaving you.' He made it plain.

'I'll kill myself,' she sniffled. 'I'll jump off a cliff before I let him get me again.'

'That ain't no way to talk, Miss Dorothy,' Ben remonstrated.

'But we're two against the Lord knows how many,' she cried.

He didn't trouble himself pointing out that they were, in fact, one against the Lord knew how many and that she was no use at all.

'Quite clearly we need to kill every one of them,' she mused, unexpectedly calming.

'Well, that figures,' he drawled, wondering how the hell he was going to manage the destruction of the entire band.

'Who is Concita?' Miss Dorothy demanded.

Ben was amazed she could ask such a question now of all times.

'You were muttering in your sleep,' she explained.

'You must have mighty keen ears, Miss Dorothy,' Ben rejoined, damned if he was going to reply further.

'I often wondered . . . ' Her voice trailed away. 'And I'm sure you did . . . '

'No such thing, Miss Dorothy,' Ben replied quickly.

A lone steer emerged from cover, bawled and went on its way. Ben was glad of the interruption. He felt uneasy.

'This could be our last day alive, surely . . . ' she essayed.

'Well, I can't manage it, Miss Dorothy, which ain't surprising considering you arranged a lynching party for me,' he snapped.

To his surprise, she glared at him. 'You'd better damn well manage, Benjamin.' She paused. 'I've hit upon a plan to save us. I know how we can dispose of Amigo and the rest of them.'

'You do?' he drawled in disbelief.

'Unless you can think of something you'd better get over here . . . '

'What's your plan, Miss Dorothy?' he asked, not that he considered her crazy plan would be worth much.

'Later,' she replied firmly. 'And don't you dare say this is not the time or place. We haven't much time left if we don't come up with a plan. Well, I have. But you need to carry it out.'

'Hell.' He took a step towards her. He was desperate enough to humour her. He'd just have to close his eyes and think of Concita, he told himself.

★ ★ ★

Amigo's tracker picked up the trail of the gringo and the woman. The two rode not towards the border but deeper into Mexico as they headed upwards into the mountain range.

Amigo laughed. 'If the gringo thinks

to hide from me then he is a fool,'
he announced, as he rode behind his
tracker, the man having dismounted
preferring for now to hunt on foot,
moccasin-shod feet moving fast as his
eyes skimmed the rocky ground.

★ ★ ★

Miss Dorothy's plan such as it was,
she readily admitted, had come out of
a dime novel. But she didn't see, she
explained, why it could not work. And
if he could think of a better way than
he only had to say so.

The hell of it was that, of course,
he could not think of a thing. And
she was right: her plan might just
work. So, with Ben leading, they began
to wend their way downwards. They
moved slowly, Ben afraid that one of
the horses might slip. Riderless, or with
one horse between them, they would be
in dire straits. He held on to that fact
and refused to rush.

Whatever kind of woman she was,

she was certainly a brave one to risk falling into Amigo's clutches again. Especially as she knew what the bandit had in store for her.

Ben knew he must have managed a darn sight too well, for Miss Dorothy's face wore a happy smile and every now and again she bestowed a glance upon him which warned him she was getting ideas.

It would not, Ben thought, cross Amigo's mind that he and Miss Dorothy intended to make a stand. The idea was plain ridiculous. But that was what they were going to do. He would have preferred to face Amigo alone, man to man, with the faster man emerging as victor. Ben was confident. He truly believed that he was the better man. That he could haul iron faster than Amigo. But Amigo would never let it be that simple. Amigo rode with his own personal army at his back. And he was out to get Ben any way he could. Which left Ben without a choice. He must go after Amigo and his men any way that seemed possible.

'It's possible, isn't it?' Miss Dorothy had asked. And he'd assured her that it was. He hadn't bothered to add that time was running out for them both fast. She knew it.

★ ★ ★

To Amigo's disbelief, the gringo had decided to abandon his flight upwards into the mountains in favour of descending and making a run for the border.

Frowning slightly, Amigo followed the downward trail as it twisted and turned, heading towards the land owned by his brother.

Amigo quirted his horse unwilling to slow his pace despite the risk. He had time to make up. Time wasted in ambushing De Bois. Alas, De Bois had escaped true retribution for he had been killed instantly.

But not the gringo. 'I want him alive,' Amigo screeched. 'I want this gringo alive. I want to hear him scream for mercy.' He paused. 'The mad woman is not important.' Crow had destroyed everything and with seeming ease. Even now it was hard to believe the damage the elusive Crow had managed to wreak.

★ ★ ★

'I'll be seeing you, Miss Dorothy,' Ben touched the brim of his hat. He just hoped they were not destined to meet up again in Hell.

She nodded. 'Dear Benjamin. I'm sure we have many years before us.'

'We don't, Miss Dorothy, we don't,' he responded desperately. 'Well, it just wouldn't be right. Meaks has loved you from afar for many years. It ain't fitting I step on his toes.'

'Meaks!'

Ben prayed Meaks was in Mexico searching for her. Hell, that was one good reason not to blast Meaks. The man was fool enough to take the murderously inclined Miss Dorothy. Ben would take a Concita any day. It was safer.

Leading the horses, Ben left Miss Dorothy sitting on the ground. At least if she had Meaks to think about it might keep her thoughts from Amigo the man-burner.

To give Miss Dorothy her due, all was as she had said it would be. The woman possessed a keen eye and a memory for detail.

★ ★ ★

All this, Amigo thought bitterly, should now be mine. He gazed at the grazing cattle. They obscured his view of the canyon. Beyond that canyon lay a flat, open stretch of land which led down to the river. How often had he ridden this way? Many times, more times than he could remember.

He urged his horse forward into the canyon known as the Bottle Neck for one side was wide and the other narrow.

They were not very far ahead now so his tracker assured him. Perhaps just beyond the mouth of the Bottle Neck.

'She is there, Amigo!' His tracker pointed. His lieutenant raised a rifle.

'No,' Amigo knocked the rifle from the man's hand. 'We will burn her. And then we will find Crow. His fate will not be so merciful.' He laughed. At the end, Crow had abandoned the woman as he sought to save his own skin. She sat alone rocking back and forth as a mad woman might do.

Obviously spotting him, Miss Dorothy scrambled to her feet and ran, not towards the mouth of the Bottle Neck, but towards one of the sheer walls.

Ben raised his Colt. He fired. And then fired again as the cattle started to move forward, quickly picking up speed as he banged his frying pan with a spoon. Bawling, they streamed into the canyon. Soon he could see nothing as the cloud of choking red dust stirred by countless hooves enveloped him.

Miss Dorothy squeezed her lanky body into the fissure, taking care to pull in her skirts. She closed her eyes as the shots rang out and the bawling commenced. The ground seemed to shake as the cattle thundered into the canyon.

Amigo looked at the wall of death which fast approached. And he looked at the mouth of the Bottle Neck and was able to see even from a distance that the devil Crow had thought to block the mouth. Every shrub hereabouts had been piled across the narrow opening. His enemy had won. Around him, men screamed. He screamed himself without even realizing it. He screamed the name of his enemy.

Meaks found Crow amidst the carnage of the canyon. Mangled steers, horses and what once had been men dotted the blood-soaked ground.

'There's some would say Miss Dorothy deserves to hang,' Crow stated without preamble.

'Well, I ain't one of them,' Meaks replied stoutly. 'Do you want satisfaction?'

Suddenly Crow smiled. 'Why the hell would I want satisfaction, Meaks?' he taunted. 'I don't want to kill you.' He had a good reason not to kill Pat Meaks. 'She's alive.' He jerked his head. 'And waiting for you.'

As for himself maybe he'd look up Concita — after he'd buried the two gunny sacks Miss Dorothy kept insisting he take.

'If I've got Miss Dorothy I ain't done badly,' Meaks muttered.

To Meaks's surprise Crow winked. 'Me neither, Meaks,' he said, as he thought of the contents of the sacks. 'Me neither.'

## THE END

# RIDERS OF RIFLE RANGE
## Wade Hamilton

Veterinarian Jeff Jones did not like open warfare — but it was there on Scrub Pine grass. When he diagnosed a sick bull on the Endicott ranch as having the contagious blackleg disease, he got involved in the warfare — whether he liked it or not!

# BEAR PAW
## Nevada Carter

Austin Dailey traded two cows to a pair of Indians for a bay horse, which subsequently disappeared. Tracks led to a secret hideout of fugitive Indians — and cattle thieves. Indians and stockmen co-operated against the rustlers. But it was Pale Woman who acted as interpreter between her people and the rangemen.

## THE WEST WITCH
### Lance Howard

Detective Quinton Hilcrest journeys west, seeking the Black Hood Bandits' lost fortune. Within hours of arriving in Hags Bend, he is fighting for his life, ensnared with a beautiful outcast the town claims is a witch! Can he save the young woman from the angry mob?


## GUNS OF THE PONY EXPRESS
### T. M. Dolan

Rich Zennor joined the Pony Express venture at the start, as second-in-command to tough Denning Hartman. But Zennor had the problems of Hartman believing that they had crossed trails in the past, and the fact that he was strongly attached to Hartman's Indian girl, Conchita.

## BLACK JO OF THE PECOS
### Jeff Blaine

Nobody knew where Black Josephine Callard came from or whither she returned. Deputy U.S. Marshal Frank Haggard would have to exercise all his cunning and ability to stay alive before he could defeat her highly successful gang and solve the mystery.

## RIDE FOR YOUR LIFE
### Johnny Mack Bride

They rode west, hoping for a new start. Then they met another broken-down casualty of war, and he had a plan that might deliver them from despair. But the only men who would attempt it would be the truly brave — or the desperate. They were both.

## THE NIGHTHAWK
### Charles Burnham

While John Baxter sat looking at the ruin that arsonists had made of his log house, a stranger rode into the yard. Baxter and Walt Showalter partnered up and re-built the house. But when it was dynamited, they struck back — and all hell broke loose.

## MAVERICK PREACHER
### M. Duggan

Clay Purnell was hopeful that his posting to Capra would be peaceable enough. However, on his very first day in town he rode into trouble. Although loath to use his .45, Clay found he had little choice — and his likeness to a notorious bank robber didn't help either!

## SIXGUN SHOWDOWN
### Art Flynn

After years as a lawman elsewhere, Dan Herrick returned to his old Arizona stamping ground to find that nesters were being driven from their homesteads by ruthless ranchers. Before putting away his gun once and for all, Dan forced a bloody and decisive showdown.

## RIDE LIKE THE DEVIL!
### Sam Gort

Ben Trunch arrived back on the Big T only to find that land-grabbing was in progress. He confronted Luke Fletcher, saloon-keeper and town boss, with what was happening, and was immediately forced to ride for his life. But he got the chance to put it all right in the end.